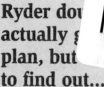

Ryder dou **actually** **plan, but** **to find out…**

"I think we should do a test," he said. "To see if we're compatible, sexually speaking."

Her eyes widened. "You mean…now?"

"Relax, Sam. I'm only talking about a kiss. Did you think I intended to toss you into the back seat of your car and jump you?" When she didn't answer, he continued. "It's just a kiss," he said, slipping his arm around her waist. "A simple little kiss."

But the kiss turned out to be anything but simple. Ryder had kissed a lot of women in his time, but he'd never felt such an instantaneous rush of heat. It was like being hit by lightning. Oh yeah, definite electricity. Stunned and a little disoriented, he pulled back.

"Wow," Sam whispered. "So does this mean…"

"I'm still thinking." He was thinking, all right. About the two of them together, doing things she'd probably never dreamed of. About that needy little moan she'd let out when he touched her. It wasn't much of a leap to fantasize about her bucking beneath him in the throes of a wild climax. He was already hard.

And he was definitely thinking about taking her up on her offer….

Dear Reader,

What do you get when you take one wild cowboy trying to be good, then add one good girl trying to be bad? One hot combination, that's what!

My hero, Ryder Wells, is hell-bent on saving his ranch, even if he has to cut a deal with the devil. And while banker Samantha Collins knows all about deals and dollars, she knows very little about men. But, oh boy, is she willing to learn....

So what else can Sam do but use her knowledge of figures as a trade-off in a deal Ryder can't refuse? After all, in this equation, one lady with questions plus one sexy cowboy with the right answers could add up to "two" hot to handle....

Sit back and enjoy the heat,

Sandy Steen

Books by Sandy Steen

HARLEQUIN TEMPTATION

Don't miss any of our special offers. Write to us at the following address for information on our newest releases.

Harlequin Reader Service
U.S.: 3010 Walden Ave., P.O. Box 1325, Buffalo, NY 14269
Canadian: P.O. Box 609, Fort Erie, Ont. L2A 5X3

ONE HOT NUMBER
Sandy Steen

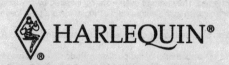

TORONTO • NEW YORK • LONDON
AMSTERDAM • PARIS • SYDNEY • HAMBURG
STOCKHOLM • ATHENS • TOKYO • MILAN • MADRID
PRAGUE • WARSAW • BUDAPEST • AUCKLAND

If you purchased this book without a cover you should be aware
that this book is stolen property. It was reported as "unsold and
destroyed" to the publisher, and neither the author nor the
publisher has received any payment for this "stripped book."

For Mom,
with all my love and thanks.

ISBN 0-373-25980-8

ONE HOT NUMBER

Copyright © 2002 by Sandy Steen.

All rights reserved. Except for use in any review, the reproduction or
utilization of this work in whole or in part in any form by any electronic,
mechanical or other means, now known or hereafter invented, including
xerography, photocopying and recording, or in any information storage
or retrieval system, is forbidden without the written permission of the
publisher, Harlequin Enterprises Limited, 225 Duncan Mill Road,
Don Mills, Ontario, Canada M3B 3K9.

All characters in this book have no existence outside the imagination of
the author and have no relation whatsoever to anyone bearing the same
name or names. They are not even distantly inspired by any individual
known or unknown to the author, and all incidents are pure invention.

This edition published by arrangement with Harlequin Books S.A.

® and TM are trademarks of the publisher. Trademarks indicated with
® are registered in the United States Patent and Trademark Office, the
Canadian Trade Marks Office and in other countries.

Visit us at www.eHarlequin.com

Printed in U.S.A.

1

"ARE YOU NERVOUS?"

"Do I look nervous?" Samantha Collins asked her friend and co-worker, Connie Tyler.

"Nope."

Sam smiled, smoothed the collar of her best and most businesslike suit. "Looking confident is half the battle. You know the motto—"

"Never let 'em see you sweat," they said in unison.

"Just between you and me," Sam told Connie, "I'm scared spitless that they took one look at my budget and decided to throw me out on my keister."

"Fat chance. You really think Anderson is going to turn loose the employee that makes him look good? He can't *not* give you the promotion, especially with the merger just around the corner."

"Sex," Sam replied.

"Excuse me?"

"My sex may work against me. Let's don't forget Anderson is a card-carrying member of the good old boys' club."

"True. And ordinarily I'd say that automatically dropped his IQ to around sixty, but he's smart enough to know that because you're hot with numbers, he doesn't dare treat you like one hot number. Your brains have saved his corporate butt more than once."

"I'm not the only one under consideration."

"No. You're just the only one generous enough to even give the other candidate a passing thought."

Sam glanced at her watch, then over the top of her cubicle at the door to Wendall Anderson's office. Anderson was not only an assistant vice president of Frontier Financial Bank and Trust, but also her immediate supervisor and the man who was about to preside over her semiannual review. "I've got to go. Wish me luck," she said and headed for his office.

WHEN SHE RETURNED forty-five minutes later, she was greeted by Connie popping her head over her cubicle. "Well?"

"Someday I hope that man gets everything he deserves."

"Like what?"

"A slow and painful death."

Connie's mouth dropped open. "You didn't get it?"

"Oh, I got something, but it definitely wasn't the promotion. In fact, there'll be no promotions until after the merger. He even showed me a memo to that effect, which meant he's been stringing me along until I finished the budget."

"What about it? Didn't they like it?"

"They liked it, all right. Anderson told me how complimentary the other VPs were about—you're going to love this—all the hard work he'd put into *his* budget report."

"What! Why, that sleazy, backbiting, good-for-nothing—"

"Don't hold back on my account."

"—son of a bitch. The man takes credit for your work then has the nerve to brag about it?"

Briefly, Sam closed her eyes as if to blot out the image of her boss grinning like an ass as he went on and on about his success. "Do I have sucker written across my forehead?" she asked her friend. "I trusted him when he told me he valued my work, couldn't run the department without me, that I was the star of his team."

"Hey, anybody that can count past ten knows you're the brains in this department. And, obviously, the guts."

"That doesn't get me a name plaque on my door. What am I saying? I don't even have a door. All I've got is a cubicle and mountains of work—mine, plus all of his." She pointed toward Anderson's office. "I should have known when he started putting me off about the promotion that something was funny."

"God, I'm sorry. Of all the people around here, you don't deserve this kind of treatment. Nobody works harder than you, Sam."

"You haven't even heard the best part. He wants me to personally reappraise a piece of property in Lewisville. Rush job. Very important. Yada, yada. The Copper Canyon file. That loan is due to be terminated within the next twenty to thirty days, and now he wants another appraisal. It seems the bank already has a potential buyer, so he wants me to leave right away."

"Today?"

"Try now."

Connie thought for a moment. "If he's in that big a hurry it wouldn't surprise me to learn the potential buyer is acquainted with our gutless leader."

"Nor me."

Connie shrugged and then smiled. "Well, keep your chin up. Things could be worse. Besides, today is payday."

FOUR HOURS LATER Sam discovered just how true it was that things could be worse. She'd cheered up, then she'd called into the office. It took only one comment from Connie to find out that things had definitely gotten worse.

"Bad news," Connie said as Sam picked up her cell phone.

"How bad?"

"You, me and a third of the staff fired. That bad enough for you?"

"Tell me you're kidding."

"I wish I could. But that remark you made this morning about being out on your keister was damn near prophetic. It's massive, Sam. The whole office is in shock."

"You're sure?"

"Saw your name on the list with my own eyes," Connie assured her. "And it's a damn long list, I might add. The bastards didn't even have the decency to be discreet. It took about thirty minutes for the news to make it from downtown to our office, and by then, they were already handing out memos. They're not even giving us two weeks to find other jobs. Whatever happened to the concept of private pink slips in pay envelopes?"

"Direct deposits," Sam said. "It's the twenty-first century."

"Damn computers."

"You can damn them all you want until it's time to e-mail your résumé. Besides, this isn't about technology, it's about greed."

"Boy, you got that right," Connie said. "And that ass Anderson didn't even have the balls to hand out the memos himself. He let some flunky from personnel do it. We all knew the merger would wipe out some jobs, but nothing like this. I'll bet they've laid off thirty percent of the Dallas employees today, and rumor has it they're not done." Connie sighed, then asked, "You okay? You're coming back in, aren't you?"

Sam massaged her right temple where a headache was blooming. "I don't think so. I had a flat right after I left the office, then my starter gave me trouble when I stopped for gas in Lewisville."

"Again? That's happened three times in the last couple of weeks."

"Yeah. I was planning on having it fixed this weekend, plus a tune-up and some other things, but now..." Sam stared at the bag of fast food she'd just picked up at a drive-through when her cell phone chirped. Suddenly, the last thing on her mind was food. "Anyway, all of that forced me to push this appraisal back to three o'clock."

"Damn. That'll put you back right in the middle of the usual Friday afternoon traffic snarl."

"A bad end to an otherwise perfect day, huh? Guess I'll wait, then come into the office to file my notes after the traffic dies down."

"No hurry now. All you have to do is clean out your desk. In fact, if I were you, I'd say screw that appraisal and just go on home."

"Don't tempt me."

"I'm sure the client wouldn't mind."

"Probably not, but that wouldn't let him, or me, off the hook. They'll just send someone else. Besides, until I'm officially notified otherwise, I still work for Frontier Financial Bank and Trust."

"I knew you were going to say something like that. You just hang in there no matter what, don't you? Too bad some of your business ethics didn't rub off on Anderson. For once I wish I was a man so I could take him out to a dark alley and..."

"He isn't worth the effort," Sam said.

There was a long sigh. "Oh, don't pay any attention to me. Going eyeball to eyeball with unemployment makes me crabby. But for God's sake, whatever you do don't say, 'Things could be worse'."

Despite the situation Sam couldn't help but grin. "So, what are your plans?"

"Comb the classifieds. Start hitting the agencies. At that, I guess I've got it a little better than you do. I'm just a secretary. You're closer to management. And I've always got my Mom and Dad to fall back on." Another long sigh. "I'm sorry, Sam. That was really thoughtless of me to mention my family when you don't have any."

"It's all right."

"I wish you at least had someone in your life right now. Some good-looking man who makes you forget about everything else."

"That makes two of us."

"Well," Connie insisted, "if we're going to dream, might as well dream big, right? No harm in that."

"None at all. Hold that thought."

Connie laughed. "Yeah. Hey, maybe we could get together for lunch after we both get settled in new jobs."

"Sure." It was a lie of reassurance, but Sam honestly didn't know who needed it the most, she or Connie.

"Well, take care of yourself, huh?"

"Thanks. You, too."

Sam hit the end button, staring at the phone for several moments before realizing she was holding her breath. *Breathe,* she told herself. *In. Out. Deep breaths.* So she'd lost her job. It wasn't the end of the world.

"Don't panic, and you'll be fine," she whispered.

To her surprise she wasn't as panicked as she'd expected. In fact, not at all. For almost a month, she and most of Frontier's North Park branch employees had been waiting for the layoffs everyone knew were inevitable. No, she wasn't panicked, she was just plain mad as hell. For five years she'd worked her tail off at Frontier and fought an uphill battle with the good old boys' club mentality, and she'd finally thought she'd seen the light at the end of the tunnel. Now she was back to square one. Maybe not square one, but there was no denying this was a setback. But Sam had never been one to wring her hands over things she couldn't change. It might take her a while to find a job, but in the meantime she could do temp work. A nicely padded savings account assured her she wouldn't starve for a while. She had a good education, experience and, most of all, tenacity. Once she made a decision, she followed through. Admittedly, it would be great to have something to fall back on—or someone. But orphans didn't have the luxury of a family, and she had worked too long and too hard to make it on her own to wallow in self-pity.

Sam glanced at the hamburger she'd paid for moments before Connie had called and realized she truly was no longer hungry. But old habits, particularly ones born out of poverty and self-reliance, die hard. She picked up the burger and took a bite. It was cold. She sighed, pitched the burger into the paper sack, deciding to keep the bag of chips for later. Waste not, want not. One of the many ingrained reprimands from her Catholic orphanage upbringing. The stern discipline she'd so abhorred as a child came in handy on days like today. Like all the other days in her life that had required a stiff upper lip and self-sacrifice. She'd been a should and ought girl all of her life. A responsible girl. A good girl. Work and responsibility were the foundations of her life. Only lately, a mild rebelliousness had been brewing in her mind. All that work and no play was definitely on the verge of making her a dull girl. Her life felt confined, stuffy and, well, boring. Not that she intended to toss her inhibitions to the wind and run wild. But a *little* wildness never hurt anybody, did it?

And now she was free, albeit temporarily, of work and responsibility.

Some might say it was pure coincidence and ignore it. Not Sam. She didn't believe in coincidence. Everything happened for a reason. And it shouldn't be ignored that she had needed a change, needed freedom, and then, out of the blue, it was practically handed to her on a silver platter. Maybe it was time to start thinking about what she *wanted* to do rather than what she *should* do. She'd been taught to be a good girl. Maybe it was time she expanded her education, spread her wings and found out what it was like to fly. Maybe it was time to go looking for... What was it Connie had said? A good-looking man who made her forget about everything else?

Lord knew, there had been no one for over eight months, and even then, to be perfectly honest, her last boyfriend, Cal, hadn't really done it for her. He was good-looking, smart, well-dressed and successful—all the things she'd always thought she wanted in a man. But they'd been together for slightly more than six months and in that time she couldn't remember the two of them ever really having fun. Cal liked moody French films, obsessed over chocolate and drank only Russian vodka, but refused it unless it was very cold and served in hand-blown crystal shot glasses. Sam almost never drank anything stronger than the wine she put into some of her favorite recipes. The ideal man he

wasn't, and after he left it hadn't taken her long to realize she was well rid of him. Looking back, she
couldn't even say he was a great lover. Not that she
had a broad basis for comparison. She'd had sex with
the underwhelming number of two men. Cal hadn't
been right for her, but somewhere the right man was
waiting, and he'd be handsome, exciting and a good
kisser, to boot. Another talent Cal had lacked. Yeah,
that was a must. She wanted a knock-your-socks-off,
curl-your-toes kind of kisser. In fact, the very next fun-
loving, exciting, make-your-toes-curl sexy man to cross
her path better look out, because she was on the look-
out.

Suddenly, thoughts of looking for the best kisser of
the century collided with her unexpected freedom and
gave birth to an idea that had some real possibilities.
She needed some excitement, and for the first time in
her life, she felt free enough to enjoy it. It was time, no,
past time, for her to fly. To find her ideal man, if such a
dream boat existed. And Sam had a hunch he was out
there waiting. He had to be. She had read somewhere
that dreams were expressions of repressed desires. If
that were true, some guy was going to get lucky beyond his wildest imagination.

She glanced at her clipboard resting beside her on
the seat. First she had to finish her job for which she
was due one last paycheck, so she put her car into gear
and headed down FM 407 into Copper Canyon, Texas,
for her appointment. It was, after all, the responsible
thing to do. Again, she wondered if Fate had taken a
hand in her future.

RYDER GLANCED UP as he walked past the corral and approached the barn, then stopped and stared at the words Copper Canyon Ranch written in rope over the double doors. How many times had he walked under those words, he wondered? Thousands. Maybe a million. But the big question was how much longer would he have that opportunity? If Frontier Bank and Trust had their way, not much longer at all.

It was barely mid-morning and already the muscles across his shoulders felt like a congregation of knots. If the tension was this bad now, he'd be ready to take the appraiser's head off by the time he arrived. Still, Ryder couldn't get past the resentment gnawing at him. Most of it directed at himself, but with plenty left over for the bank and its bloodthirsty bottom liners. He'd spent the last year and every cent of his savings to turn his family's legacy into a profitable facility similar to South Fork and Beaumont Ranch. Copper Canyon offered catering, rodeos, roundups, everything for corporate retreats and company parties. And he was close to succeeding. Bookings were coming in at a steady clip, and they had two contracts for parties large enough to put them even and enable him to catch up on the loan payments. But none of that mattered now. He'd talked to the loan officer until he was nearly blue in the face. Damn near got down on his knees and begged for an extension. All for nothing. Frontier Financial was in the process of merging with a massive conglomerate bank, and the new management wasn't interested in anything from Ryder but the money he owed. Now. All this had come to a head two days ago, and since then he'd tried to find new financing without any luck.

Not that he couldn't manage money or was afraid of hard work. He might be a cowboy, but he wasn't a dunce when it came to business. And while his education might have been more hard knocks than Harvard, he had a dead-on knack for finding the right person to make up for whatever he lacked. As a movie stuntman he'd listened, learned, then hired a top business manager. Then, after ten years of pushing himself hard and following sound financial advice, he'd made the biggest—no, make that *two* of the biggest mistakes of his life.

He fell in love. Then he let that love make him deaf, dumb and blind to the truth.

Alicia was smart, savvy, a one-time CPA and the woman of his dreams. She became his lover, his helpmate and, eventually, his business partner. Since he planned on making her a permanent part of his life what could be more natural than making her part of his business? It started casually enough with her fielding calls from his agent, then she started handling his bookings full-time. He'd trusted her so completely he hadn't hesitated when she suggested taking over his books, as well. He'd been so crazy about her he didn't see even the possibility of disaster it until it was too late. Then one morning he woke up and found her, and his money, gone. The only thing that saved him from being totally wiped out were the CDs sitting in a Texas bank that his dad had urged him to set up at the beginning of his career. That had been a little more than a year ago, and Ryder often wondered how long it might have taken him to get over the loss of love and his life savings if his dad hadn't died just then. The ranch and the people on it became his responsibility. So he did the only thing he could do. He quit the stunt business and moved back to Texas, only to discover that his dad's finances were also on shaky ground.

Through his old business manager, Ryder found a great banker and, he thought, a great bank in Frontier Financial. Then the banker retired, almost a month of steady rain forced party cancellations, and the bank merged.

Ryder could swing a rope, charm customers and manage wranglers with the best of them, but he hated the tedious, monotonous numbers end of the business. That had been the basis for the calamity with Alicia. Now he was more careful. He would never completely turn over the money handling to anyone else, but he did need someone with a good head for business, someone he could trust. He'd learned the hard way, though, that those kind of people didn't grow on trees. And for now it looked like he'd run out of time and talent. As much as he hated to admit it, he'd come to the end of his rope. Short of a miracle, he was facing foreclosure or having to sell. He was desperate, and there was nothing he wouldn't do to keep the ranch. Including make a deal with the devil.

Cotton West, ranch foreman for over twenty years, looked up from pitching hay as Ryder stomped into the barn, grabbed a pitchfork and took up the same task without a word. After a full hour of hard labor

Cotton paused, leaned on his pitchfork, and looked at Ryder. "You wanna talk about it? Get it outta yore system?"

"Talk about what?"

"The fact that yore wound up like an eight-day clock. If you don't do somethin' you're gonna blow a fuse. Get yourself in a peck a trouble."

"Don't know what you're talking about."

"The hell you don't. You're walkin' round here with a chip on yore shoulder big as Texas Stadium, jest darin' someone to knock it off."

"So what?" Ryder snapped. "If losing everything you own isn't enough to make a man testy, I don't know what is. Right now a good old-fashioned knock-down-drag-out fight would feel real good."

"A course you got a right to be testy. Not sayin' you don't. But it ain't gonna do you no good if you haul off and punch the man the bank sends. Hell, you don't need a night in jail on top of everythin' else."

"I'm not going to punch anybody."

Cotton thought for a moment, then hitched up his britches. "Reckon I'm elected then."

Ryder smiled for what felt like the first time in days. "Oh, no, you don't. I can't afford the bail money. Besides," he teased, "if we're going to jail I'd much rather it be a good fight over a bad woman, wouldn't you?"

Cotton grinned. "Now, you're talkin'."

"Don't let Mamie hear you say that. She'd nail both of our hides to the barn door."

"Damn straight. That wife a mine's a mite jealous, for sure."

"Not without cause."

"You know I done give up tomcattin' years back."

"Thanks to Mamie's cast-iron skillet."

Cotton rubbed the spot that was a permanent lump on his skull. "The woman's got a mean streak, all right."

Several minutes passed before he added, "You sure about that punch?" But before Ryder could answer Cotton held up his hand. "Hold on." He walked to the barn door and pointed to a blue sedan coming up the road leading to the Rio Grande Room, the largest entertainment facility of the ranch, situated between the barn and corral area and the main house. "We got company."

Ryder stabbed his pitchfork into a mound of hay, wiped his sweaty face with the sleeve of his T-shirt then snagged his tattered baseball cap from the post of a nearby stall. "Probably the appraiser."

"Shore makin' bankers with better-lookin' legs these days," Cotton announced as Ryder stepped past him, then stopped.

A woman got out of the blue car. A very attractive woman, he decided. This couldn't be the appraiser. The idea that the expected *he* might be a *she* had never entered his mind. If it had, she certainly wouldn't look like the woman he saw now. Cotton was definitely right. They were making bankers with better legs. Clearly, she'd tried to look all businesslike, but the way she filled out the tailored blouse, the way her short, straight skirt showed off those gorgeous long legs made it impossible. She'd missed with the shoes, too.

About three-inch heels, he guessed. And strawberry blond hair. His favorite. All in all, she was just about the sexiest package he'd seen in a long time. And Ryder knew sexy in all its flavors—blond, brunette and redhead. He might not know all the finer points of high finance, but he knew his way around a woman. A gift, his grandmother had called it, and warned it would be his undoing some day. He never dreamed how right she could be. While he definitely appreciated a tasty female, he'd learned the hard way that it was better not to overindulge.

Cotton nudged him. "She's a looker, ain't she?"

"Not bad." Bad, hell, Cotton was right on the money. She was most definitely a looker. And while his body was saying go get her, his better judgment said cool it. This woman didn't look like some buckle bunny out for a good time. And he wasn't a carefree cowboy looking to smooth talk his way into a one-night stand. Not that the idea didn't have merit, he thought, admiring the lady banker's gorgeous legs. One-night stands were a good thing, as far as he was concerned. Less hassle. Less damage control required. Yeah, if things were different... But they weren't. It was true he'd ignored certain of his physical needs lately, but this was no time to let his body call the shots.

"Say." Cotton nudged him in the ribs. "Why don't you put on yore best smile, polish up some of that sweet talk you use on the ladies and—"

"For her?"

"She's female, ain't she? Shine on up to her, and maybe she'll jest sorta forget about that appraisal."

"Are you crazy?" Ryder shook his head. "She's probably married with three kids and has a can of Mace in her purse. Besides—" he straightened his shoulders "—I'm tired of groveling. For the last week I've done almost as much beggin' as I have breathin', and where's it got me?"

"That's your pride talkin'. You got nothin' to lose. Even if she don't forget about the report maybe she can jest delay it a day or two till you can talk to some of them money men."

All right, it was pride, and Ryder knew he'd probably regret it, but he couldn't bring himself to beg again. He looked at the woman and all he saw was a reminder of the past and a hard-won lesson about never trusting women. "You sweet-talk her. I got better ways to spend my time."

"She don't wanna talk to me."

"Well, she's damn sure not gonna talk to me. We're going over there, meet her, then she's all yours," Ryder said. He settled the ball cap on his head, pulled the visor low and headed toward the lady appraiser.

SAM WATCHED as two men approached. One was tall with a thin, rangy frame and looked to be in his late fifties. Wisps of snow-white hair stuck out from beneath a sweat-stained cowboy hat that looked old enough to match the man year for year. The other man...

"Oh, my," she whispered. The other man was tall, broad-shouldered and straight out of her dreams.

Thirtyish, she guessed, the ideal age, and in great shape. Better than great. Fantastic. Well-worn jeans hugged muscular hips and thighs, and his faded green T-shirt with the John Deere tractor logo and the words Nothing Runs Like A Deere across the front only served to emphasize his chest muscles. And there was a lot to emphasize. The word *power* came to mind, and not just from his build. It was more in the way he walked, the way he held his head. It simply rolled off him in waves.

Careful what you wish for, she thought, a strange mixture of excitement and fear racing through her as he came closer. When a man better than any dream lover suddenly appears, what do you do? Shake his hand, faint or throw yourself at him? *Get a grip*, Sam reminded herself. This was a client, not a pickup.

They walked up to her and stopped. The older man gave her a nod. "Howdy."

"Uh..." She had to force herself to look away from dream boat. "Mr. Wells? I'm Samantha Collins, Frontier Financial Bank and Trust."

"And I'm Ryder Wells," said the younger man, removing his cap and offering his hand.

"Oh, uh...sorry." She took it, intending on a quick connection.

It didn't work out that way. But then, coming face to face with a dream never does. Sam wasn't sure what she'd expected, but it was nothing like this. While she had never been hit by a Mack truck and never hoped to be, suddenly she understood exactly what it must feel like. And all it took was one touch of Ryder Wells's hand on hers, one look into his eyes.

Sam glanced down and jerked her hand away. "N-nice to meet you."

"Same here."

This was no dream, she thought, but the real deal. The outrageously handsome real deal. Yes, that was a good word. Handsome enough to be on the pages of *GQ*, but much better suited for the pages of *American Horseman*. Dark hair. Rugged, healthy good looks. And killer blue eyes. And while he certainly wasn't the first outrageously handsome man she'd ever met, she couldn't remember ever reacting so strongly to a perfect stranger. So physically. Her skin tingled. But that was nothing compared to the way the rest of her body was responding. What was happening to her? Her pulse jumped. Her breathing quickened. She was light-headed, and her legs felt as if the bones had turned to rubber. And all the sensations were caused by Ryder Wells. It was as if he were emitting some strange ultra-sonic wave that called to her, unheard by human ears but so acutely tuned to her body that it vibrated through every cell, shaking her very foundation. It was terrifying.

And exhilarating.

While her heart raced, so did her mind, with the thought that here was a man who could make her—no, *was* making her forget everything but him. But she couldn't help remembering that she was about to hand him the next thing to a foreclosure notice.

"I, uh..." The tingling in her arm and several other parts of her body made it hard for her to concentrate.

"I'm sure this isn't easy for you, so, uh, I'll try and make it as brief and as painless as possible."

"I appreciate that." He also appreciated the way she looked, smelled and without a doubt the way she filled out that blouse. If he'd thought she looked good from a distance, up close she made his mouth water. Damn, but she was sexy. And, best of all, didn't seem to know it. Which, in his book, made her all the sexier. Then she captured a strand of hair tugged loose by the breeze, lifted her hand and patted it into place. The movement stretched the silk across her breasts just enough for him to make out the outline of her lacy bra and... He stared. Was that shadow her nipple? Arousal, sharp and hot, hit him like a sucker punch to the jaw. He forgot about loans and appraisals. Forgot about everything but the fact that he wanted to unbutton her blouse and see for himself what was beneath the silk and lace.

"Shall we..." Sam tried to swallow only to discover that her mouth was dry as dust. She cleared her throat. "Shall we take a look at the, uh, property?"

"What?"

The look in his eyes was so intense, so...hot, it was frightening. And stirring. "The property?"

"If, uh, you'll go with my foreman here, he'll show you around. Answer all your questions." Because he was damned sure in no condition to walk, much less answer questions.

"Whatever you wish."

She'd be shocked to know what he really wished. He was a little shocked himself at the erotic images popping in his mind like paparazzi flash bulbs. "I'll see you before you leave."

"Cotton West, ma'am," the older man announced. "Mighty pleased to meetcha."

Forcing herself to look away from Ryder's handsome face, Sam turned to the foreman. "Nice to meet you, Mr. West. And thank you," she said.

"You go on and call me Cotton." He took off his hat to reveal a head of white-as-cotton hair. "Everybody does."

"Thank you." Gratefully, she followed the foreman.

Ryder watched them walk toward the barn and wondered if he'd lost his mind. He'd reacted to Samantha Collins like a stallion with his first scent of mare in heat. What the hell was wrong with him, lusting after the appraiser? It had to be him, because from where he stood there was absolutely nothing wrong with her. That body. And that face. All right, so he barely made it to her face, but she was beautiful. Her skin put satin to shame. Her hair begged to be touched. Of course, instead of being caught at the back of her neck with a barrette, it would look better loose, sorta dancing around her shoulders. Better still, spread out on a pillow, tangled in his hands...

Ryder ran his hands over his face. He had to get a grip on himself. He had enough trouble on his plate without going stupid over a woman. But he tortured himself with one last look at the enticing sway of Samantha Collins's hips and her long legs as she strolled beside Cotton. It was tough, but Ryder finally managed to pull his gaze from the sight and walk away.

"Well, now, Miz Collins," Cotton said, as they approached the barn. "Reckon you wanna take a look around."

"It's Miss and, yes, I'd like to see what improvements have been made since the last appraisal."

The foreman smiled, touched the brim of his hat and offered her his arm. "Well, you jest latch on to old Cotton. I'll tell you everything you wanna know."

Forty-five minutes later Sam had a page and a half of notations, photos of the property and an excellent idea of what Ryder Wells had attempted to do with his guest ranch. The facility had been set up to accommodate parties ranging in size from fifty to three or four hundred people. The main house was reserved for Ryder's living quarters, with a small one-bedroom cottage at the back for Cotton and his wife. There was a bunkhouse for six of the eight regular employees, four guest bunkhouses large enough to accommodate six to eight people for an overnight stay and a small outdoor arena for rodeos. Next to the corral was the main facility, called the Rio Grande Room, a fifteen-thousand-square-foot building complete with a bandstand, full kitchen and wide patio. He had some great ideas but, unfortunately, it appeared the execution fell short of success, but she couldn't quite put her finger on why. Cotton had just finished showing her the last item on his list, a couple of crossbred longhorn cows about ready to calve.

"Thank you for your time, Cotton. I'm sure you had better things to do than baby-sit me."

"Don't mind at all, Miz Collins. Shoot—" he gave

her a shy grin "—for a fella on the ripe side of sixty it's a downright event to get to spend time with a purdy lady."

They stopped at the corral where several young men were working with some horses. "Are those employees?"

"Hel—heck no. Jest a bunch of high school kids. They come out two, three times a week wantin' to pick up a few points from Ryder. Reckon they fancy themselves stuntmen."

"Stuntmen?"

"Yes, ma'am. That's what Ryder used to do." He gestured toward her clipboard. "Ain't that in your papers?"

"No."

"Well, sure. He spent ten years doin' stunts out there in Hollywood. Got to be real good at it, too. Did them pictures with all them big action stars like that Rocky fella and Arnold what's-his-name."

"Schwarzenegger."

"That's the one," he told her with pride. "Yessir, he lived high, wide and handsome, he did. Always sendin' pictures of him and his buddies from all over the world. Racin' cars, divin' like in them Jock Custoe specials. And always with lots of them, whaddayacallit, beautiful people." He winked. "Mostly women. I reckon they liked bein' close to dangerous men."

Sam didn't doubt that at all. She'd been close enough to the man to testify that he radiated a powerful mixture of danger and sex appeal.

"Reckon he'd still be at it if his daddy hadn't died 'bout a year back."

"Oh, I'm sorry to hear that."

"Yeah. It was hard. He promised his daddy on his deathbed to stay and work the ranch, and that's 'xactly what he's done. He come home, took a hold and done his best. He ain't stupid, mind you, but I gotta admit keepin' books and dealin' with bankers and such ain't his long suit. But that boy's worked his butt off—scuse me, ma'am—to make his daddy proud."

"I can see that."

"Had his share of bad breaks, for sure. 'Course, that woman runnin' off with most of his money like she did didn't help."

"Woman?"

"Happened 'fore he come back. Reckon he thought she was just about it." Cotton shook his head. "Men don't think too straight round a purdy woman sometimes. Anyways, she cleaned him out. Took ever thang but the gold in his teeth. Not that it turned him hard," he said. "Nobody loves a good time more'n Ryder, but he don't shy away from responsibility, for all the good it's done him." Cotton crammed both hands into his pockets and glanced at his boots. When he looked up he cleared his throat. "That was outta line and I'm right sorry, Miz Collins. None of this is your fault. Yore jest doin' your job is all."

"Doing my job doesn't prevent me from feeling bad about what's happening here."

"Now, don't get me wrong. Ryder ain't lookin' for no sympathy. He knew the odds when he rolled the dice. He's hit a couple a rough spots is all. Most not even his fault. If we hadn't had one of the wettest springs in recent times, probably wouldn't even be havin' this here conversation. Damned—danged if it didn't get wet early and stay that way. Had two big cancellations on account of the rain. It's jest a da—darn shame, that's for certain."

"How long has Mr. Wells's family owned this land?"

"Ryder's grandfather bought this place before World War Two. Started out with quarter horses, a few cattle. That was back in the days when there was still a few real cowboys around and a need for good workin' horses."

Sam rested her clipboard on the rail, sat her camera on top of it and gazed over the corral. Air still damp from recent rains mingled with the aromas of horse, rider and dust. To her surprise she liked the earthy smell. It didn't take much of an imagination to conjure an image of cowboys in chaps and spurs breaking horses. Of spring evenings, starry skies and a peaceful sense of belonging. She took a deep breath. Being able to recall your family history, knowing you came from solid stock and that you've always had a place to call home sounded like the best of all possible worlds to Sam. "This may sound funny under the circumstances, but I envy him."

Cotton looked a bit puzzled but asked, "You got any more questions, ma'am?"

"No. I think I've got everything I need." She smiled. "Thanks, Cotton."

"My pleasure, for sure. You wait right here while I go and get Ryder." And he walked off.

There was a part of her that would just as soon leave without seeing Ryder Wells again. He made her nervous and excited at the same time, and she wasn't sure how to deal with that. *Stay professional,* she told herself. *Cool, businesslike, even aloof.* But a few moments later when he came out of the main house with Cotton and walked toward her, she knew it wasn't going to be easy to remain aloof from Ryder Wells. The man all but shouted sex and power with every step.

"Miss Collins."

"Mr. Wells."

"If I seemed rude before—" he crammed his hands in his back pockets "—I want to apologize."

"It's all right. If it's any comfort, I wish circumstances were different."

"Nice of you to say so." Then he smiled.

Oh, my, she thought. He had one of those smiles a woman comes across once in a great while that will live in her memory forever. Slow as a Southern breeze, sure as the rising sun and sexy beyond her wildest dreams, she couldn't do anything but stare at his mouth.

"Well," he said, "I just didn't want you to go away thinking I was angry with you."

"Th-thanks."

"After all, you had nothing to do with turning down my request for an extension."

"I didn't realize you'd asked for one."

Ryder nodded curtly, feeling very little hope based on the way she was acting. She wouldn't even meet his eye. "I've got a lead on additional capital, but it'll probably be several weeks before I can pull it all together." If at all, he thought grimly.

"Under the circumstances it's only natural that you might feel resentful."

"Resentful?" The smile vanished. He was about to lose his ranch and he couldn't take it anymore. "How about just plain old pissed? You wouldn't even be here if you people had been reasonable about the extension. Not like I'm some deadbeat, for God's sake. I don't need your sympathy, Miss Collins. What I need is a financial wizard. A magician who can turn debits into credits, losses into profits. And I don't care if I have to make a deal with the devil to get it." The flare of temper was unreasonable but, dammit, she'd rattled him, and he didn't like it.

"I told you I didn't realize—"

"As far as I'm concerned you can go back and tell those sons of bitches you work for they can appraise till they're blue in the face, and I don't give a tinker's damn. This is Wells land and it's going to stay Wells land." Again, he knew he was being unreasonable, but he couldn't stop. Every day the reality of losing the ranch edged closer. So did desperation. The fear that he would probably have to sell to meet his obligations stalked the dark corners of his mind like an animal waiting to devour him. He had to find a way, any way to save the ranch.

"Don't use that tone of voice, Mr. Wells. I'm merely—"

"Yeah, I know." His hands balled into fists, and he

fought to control the rage that always threatened to overtake him when he was faced with losing something he loved. And the ranch had become his heart. "You're just an employee doing your job. Well, I gotta tell you, lady, your job sucks."

She stared at him. "You're really quite an ass once you put your mind to it, aren't you? Do you always apologize with one breath, then insult with the next?"

He blinked, too surprised to respond. "Well, let me tell you something, Mr. Wells," she continued. "My job may suck, but so does your attitude. If this is how you handled your guests, it's no wonder your business is going under." And, with that, she turned on her heels and headed for her car.

"Damn," Ryder muttered, ashamed of himself. "Miss Collins!"

Sam cut him off with a wave of dismissal and kept walking. Without looking back she got into her car and slammed the door. Out of the corner of her eye she thought she saw him stomp off toward the barn. She jabbed her key into the ignition and turned it.

Nothing. No sound. Not even a tiny whir of response.

"Oh, no, not now." She tried again. And again. Still nothing. She pumped the accelerator, knowing it wouldn't help. "Please, please." But the car wouldn't start.

Sam got out, glanced around for the foreman, Cotton. The sum total of what she knew about cars could be inscribed on the head of a straight pin, but she'd be damned if she'd ask Ryder Wells for help. Not that he would offer after her little outburst. Cotton was no-where in sight. Well, she would just have to call a wrecker and face what would probably be a horren-dous bill. Resigned, she reached to open her car door...and realized she had locked her cell phone and keys inside.

This had to be the worst day of her life. Out of sheer frustration, Sam took the first avenue of revenge she could think of against the ungrateful hunk of worthless metal. She kicked it, repeatedly, and ended up with a doozy of a run in her last good pair of stockings.

Cotton found her leaning against her car, shaking her head.

"You all right, Miz Collins?"

She glanced up. "I hate this car." A wave of hair had worked its way out of place and hung over one eye. She blew it away, but it fell right back. "Will you do me a favor and blow it up?"

"Whoa, there." Cotton grinned. "Let's see what the problem is 'fore we get so drastic."

"It's the starter," she told him. "I've been having trouble with it."

Cotton scratched his head, causing his hat to shift to one side. "I don't know much about cars, but now Ry-der—"

"Oh, no. Not him."

"He's sorta handy with—"

"Believe me, I'm the last person Mr. Wells would be interested in helping right now. I'm afraid I said some things to him that I shouldn't have."

"Well, then, you belong to one of them car clubs

that'll haul you to a garage?" When she shook her head
Cotton put a hand on her shoulder. "Now, don't you
worry. You jest c'mon with ol' Cotton, and we'll figure
out something." He escorted her to the patio of the Rio
Grande Room, sat her at one of the glass-topped tables
with a big umbrella.

"There, now. Ain't that better?"

"Thanks."

"Me and Ryder usually sit here and have a beer long
'bout this time of day. Talk about things, plans for tomorrow. You know, sorta unwind." He snapped his
fingers. "Say, how'd you like a drink? A beer?"

"I'm not much of a drinker."

"Well, hell, I ain't much of a bartender. Jest step in
once in a while when there's a big crowd. How 'bout
something with fruit juice? Put the roses back in yore
cheeks."

Sam hardly realized he was gone before he was
back. "Here you go, missy. Fix you right up. Didn't
have no fruit juice."

"What's that?"

"A Bloody Mary. We keep a bottle of mix in the icebox. Jest tomato juice with hardly any booze in it at all.
Drink up. Make you feel better."

Sam put the glass to her lips, tasting the salt around
the rim a split second before the spicy liquid hit her
throat. She swallowed and coughed.

"Too spicy?"

She shook her head. "Maybe a little."

"I can get you somethin' else if—"

"No, no." By this time the liquid had hit her stomach

and beelined to her almost virgin bloodstream. "It's...okay." Actually, it was more than okay. It was very pleasant, warm. She was beginning to feel better and took another drink.

"Now, you jest sit here a spell while I hunt up Ryder—"

"Please, I don't want you to bother him. Isn't there a garage I can call?"

"Probably. But Ryder's the one looks after the cars and trucks and such." He patted her on the shoulder then walked off saying, "Be back in a jiffy."

Sam didn't even have time to protest. What the hell, she decided. He would probably be glad to help just to be rid of her. She took a long drink of the Bloody Mary, which was tasting better with each sip. Unaccustomed to liquor, she knew to go easy. Sam knew she wasn't getting drunk, but she was feeling relaxed. With a sigh, she settled more comfortably into her chair. Yes, definitely more relaxed. Enough so that rushing back to the office to turn in her notes had lost its urgency. She had no intention of ignoring her responsibilities, but what was the hurry to clean out her desk? In fact, the more she thought about it, the less anxious and more relieved she felt. It reminded her of that first flush of freedom she used to experience the last hour of the last day of the school year. Delicious.

Of course, she had to find another job. But for the first time in a long time, the tension she'd always thought accompanied the drive for success was fading. She could almost feel the knots in her muscles relaxing. Maybe this layoff wasn't necessarily a negative. God knew, she hadn't had a vacation in forever. Maybe fate really had taken a hand in her future. Maybe it was time she appraised her life.

If she didn't rush headlong into the dog-eat-dog corporate world she would survive. Along with her savings, she had a piece of land just outside McKinney. Five undeveloped acres that she'd paid off monthly over a six-year period and that had appreciated steadily. In fact, she'd received several calls from various real estate agents with buyers offering considerably more than she'd paid for it, but she'd declined. Someday she would build her dream house there. But that was the distant future. Right now, job or no job, car or no car, Sam realized she needed some time for herself. A vacation. Some fun. She reached behind her head, unhooked the barrette holding her hair and shook it free. As free as she felt. She'd been wrong to hesitate throwing caution to the wind. That's exactly what she wanted to do. Should do. She needed to run wild. Get a tattoo. Have a hot fling...

Sam sat up in her chair. Why not? She was a healthy, unattached female with a reasonably good body. Why not have a hot fling? But not with just anybody. What she needed was a man like Ryder Wells. No, what she needed *was* Ryder Wells. As soon as the thought formed in her head Sam knew it was right. *He* was right. Exactly what she needed and—unless her raging hormones had fried her gray matter—she was exactly what he needed. Or, at least, her skill with numbers.

A business arrangement.

It was within her abilities, partially due to an overburdened, unorganized system at Frontier, to delay the appraisal. Maybe even make it disappear altogether. At the very least she could buy him some time. They each had something the other needed, so why not strike a deal? Delaying the appraisal for a hot fling. Her brains for his bed. He needed a magician with numbers, and she wanted a man. Abracadabra.

2

"THAT'S THE MOST off the wall, out of the question..."
she told herself.

But Sam couldn't stop thinking about the idea. And
with it the most delicious, erotic images danced across
her mind. Her, naked and in a tangle with Ryder, their
bodies slick with heat and sex. The two of them in a
bed, wrapped around each other, their bodies damp,
needy and driven by raw passion. Sex. Wild, hot...

She was losing her mind, wasn't she? She'd never
done anything like this in her life. Not that she hadn't
thought about it. But that was just fantasy. Dream stuff.
What she was thinking about was an out-and-out affair. But that sounded so tawdry, wanton. The truth
was it was more than wanton. It was downright bold, if
not a little calculating.

A business deal.

She almost laughed out loud at the lunacy of having
an affair with a man she didn't even call by his first
name. And that's probably exactly how he would react
if she was insane enough to approach him with her
deal. And why wouldn't he? It was ludicrous. At best,
he would probably look on it as sleeping with the en-
emy. He had little use for her sticking her nose into his

business, so there was no reason in the world he should want her in his bed.

All of which was true, but took a back seat to the thought of turning her fantasies into reality. Even the fact that he was a stranger only added to the fantasy. And no matter how she tried to dismiss the notion of an affair, it persisted.

As ideas went, she admitted hers had a few flaws, beginning with the question of whether or not she could actually deliver her end of the deal. But the idea also had merit. In a crazy, backhanded kind of way, it was even logical. She could name at least a half dozen people with enough money and inclination to invest in Ryder's business, and she certainly had the experience, with some legal help, to put such a deal together. Of course, getting him to trust her abilities after his experience with a greedy girlfriend might not be easy. Then again, she didn't want to be his girlfriend, and no money would change hands. Realistically, a business deal between the two of them was a win-win situation. A straightforward barter. It made sense. It could work. For her part, it was certainly no different, or more random, than walking into a bar, making a play for a man then going home with him. Not that she'd ever done that, either, but she knew lots of women did.

It was unorthodox, a little crazy and a lot naughty. But on the plus side, what did she have to lose? The worst Ryder could say was no. But what if he didn't? What if he actually went for the idea? Hadn't he said he was ready to make a deal with the devil to get what he wanted? How much more desperate could a man get?

Sam wasn't the devil, but there was definitely some sin in her plan, and hell to pay if anything went wrong. But what could go wrong if all the rules were spelled out right from the start? After all, it wasn't like she was asking for an engagement ring or asking him to trade his soul. Just his body. She wasn't even asking for romance. Well, she thought, a little romance couldn't hurt, but it wasn't a deal breaker. Granted, she didn't have a lot of sexual experience, but if she believed the media and popular fiction, most men would jump at the chance for such a deal. But would Ryder?

In this case presentation was important, and of course it would help if he found her attractive, desirable. Then she remembered the way he'd looked at her the moment they met, the way his gaze had felt like a heated touch and decided that might not even be an issue. But the bottom line was Ryder's depth of desperation. How bad did he want help?

She was jerked out of her thoughts when Cotton stepped onto the patio and announced, "Can't find Ryder nowheres, but don't you worry none. I sent one of the boys to hunt him down." He noticed her glass was almost empty and laid a hand on her shoulder. "Go easy, now. Wouldn't want you to hate me in the mornin'."

"No. That's my job," said a voice from behind Cotton.

Sam looked up, then around Cotton's slender frame to see a petite older woman, her salt-and-pepper hair knotted on top of her head, hands on her hips and a mean look in her eyes.

"Mamie, darlin'," Cotton exclaimed, jerking his hand away from Sam. "C'mon over here and meet Miz Collins. She's from the bank."

Mamie West stepped closer, mumbling, "Bank, my butt."

"She got ready to leave and her car won't start."

"Well, tell her to call a mechanic."

"Now, sugar. I'm jest bein' hospitable while one of the boys goes to fetch Ryder."

"Jest see you remember you're a married man."

Sam almost sputtered into her drink at the implication. But in a way it was sweet. She stood up and offered her hand. "I'm Samantha Collins, Mrs. West, and I'm afraid I'm being a real nuisance. Your husband was kind enough to keep me company while we wait for Mr. Wells."

"What's wrong with your car?" Mamie asked.

She shrugged. "The silly thing is dead as a doornail."

The conversation was so ordinary, so mundane, it made her realize her flights of fantasy about offering herself to Ryder were just that. She was still shaking her head over her temporary insanity when Ryder came through the doors of the Rio Grande Room to the patio. One look at him and all she could think of was finding the right moment to make her proposition.

The last person Ryder expected to see was Samantha Collins. He'd been relieved to think of her as gone. Now here she was, just as tempting as ever.

"What's going on?"

"Her car's dead." Mamie pointed at her husband. "And he's been talkin' her ear off."

"Crazy old woman. Jest a minute ago you were all bent outta shape cause—"

"Okay, okay." Ryder was accustomed to Mamie and Cotton's verbal volleys and knew they could get out of hand. "I'll take a look at her car."

"Uh, that may be a problem."

Until then, Ryder had avoided looking directly at Sam. When he did, he wished he hadn't. Her hair was loose, and the breeze had given it a soft ruffle. She looked soft, sleepy-eyed and so damned sexy. "Problem?"

"I'm embarrassed to admit I locked my keys inside my car."

Ryder glanced away. "Probably because I made you mad." He looked at her. "I apologize. Again."

"So do I. I never should have—"

Ryder held up his hand. "How about we just say we're even and leave it at that?"

Sam smiled. "Works for me."

"Let's go take a look," he said, and the two of them headed for her car.

Thirty minutes, a coat hanger and jumper cables later, Ryder pulled his head from underneath the hood of her car. "Think you're gonna have to have that starter replaced."

"I was afraid of that. Actually, I was planning on having it worked on this weekend, then I found out the bank laid a lot of people off today, myself included, so

I scratched that idea. Now..." she sighed. "Looks like I have no choice."

"I'm sorry about your job."

"Well—" she grinned "—it sucked anyway, didn't it?"

She had gumption. He liked that. And to his amazement, he discovered he liked Samantha Collins. Anyone that could lose their job, face major car repairs in one day and still have a sense of humor was okay in his book. His powerful—and he had to admit, a little frightening—physical reaction to her hadn't left much room for something as ordinary as liking her. That, too, was unnerving. He'd been so careful not to get emotionally involved with any woman since returning to Texas. When he was with a woman, he'd kept it strictly physical and on his terms. Samantha Collins was different. And while he liked her, he wasn't sure he liked that difference.

"Sounds like your day's gone in the can like mine."

"I'd say that's an understatement."

He pulled a handkerchief from his back pocket and wiped his hands. "So, now what?"

Well, there was the sixty-four-thousand-dollar question. She could forget her wild ideas of wild flings and go back to being a good girl. All she had to do was smile pleasantly and say something mundane like, "Thanks, I'll figure it out." But that wasn't what she wanted to say. Or do. There was no drumroll, no trumpet's blare, but Sam felt the enormity of the moment nonetheless. Stay or go. Yes or no. And when her heart whispered, *Go for it*, she listened and obeyed.

"That may depend on you," she said, suddenly feeling totally calm, focused.

He shook his head. "I don't get it."

"I'd like to talk to you about making a deal."

"A deal?"

"Yes, a mutually—" she almost said satisfying, but decided that was a little too much "—beneficial business arrangement. I think—no, I'm positive I can help you with your current financial troubles."

"Miss Collins—"

"I know that sounds presumptuous, but it's true. I may be able to help you avoid foreclosure, maybe even get you some fresh capital. Most important, I can delay your appraisal."

The whole thing was just crazy, but it did snag and hold his attention. He leaned against her car, crossed one foot in front of the other and folded his arms. "Just out of curiosity, why would you do that?"

"That's my part of the deal."

"And my part would be...what?"

It was time to go for broke. "Sex."

"Excuse me?"

"Your part of the deal would be to have sex with me. For a week. Maybe two," she said, deciding to hedge her bet.

Predictably, he laughed. "How many of those Bloody Marys did you have?"

"Only one. I'm not drunk and I'm not joking, Mr. Wells."

"Under the circumstances, don't you think you

could manage to call me by my first name?" he said, still grinning.

"All right, Ryder."

He stared at her, not sure if she was trying to be funny, or if she was plain wacko. Finally, he decided she might be a little wacko, and the best way to handle it was to go along with her until he could get her out of here. He grinned. "Well, that's a mighty tempting offer, and I'm flattered, but—"

"I'm serious about this."

"Just for the sake of argument, what makes you think I would agree to such a deal?"

"Because you need me. This ranch is all you have, and you're desperate to hang on to it. And I can't blame you."

All humor fled. She was treading dangerous ground, his private business. He straightened, pushed away from the car. "Look, Miss Collins—"

"Sam. Everybody calls me Sam."

"Well, Sam, what I need and what I don't need are none of your business. Now, you might think because you have details on the loan—"

"I know why you needed the loan in the first place. Cotton told me what happened...while you were in California."

"Cotton has a big mouth."

Despite the nerves dancing in her stomach like cold water on a hot griddle, Sam smiled. "That's possible, but it doesn't change the facts. Look, it's simple, really. You need someone with a head for figures and who knows about financial networking. I have a double degree in business management and accounting. And I've got experience in loan processing and underwriting. It may sound like bragging, but I'm good with numbers. Very good. I'm not just an appraiser. My boss only handed me this assignment because he needed it in a hurry. I also have a lot of substantial connections with money. Not millions, but enough for what you need. And there's another plus. I might be able to make the appraisal go away, and I know for certain I can delay it. Without it, the whole foreclosure process is dead in the water."

For the first time she had his full attention, and it occurred to him that she might not be a wacko after all.

"How do I know you can do what you say?"

"You can check it out."

He thought for a moment then shook his head. "It's crazy. Besides, I'm not wild about the idea of having a woman mess around in my business."

"I can understand that, but—"

"I don't trust most women when it comes to money."

"Well, I'm not most women."

"That's an understatement."

"And I'm not asking you to turn over your affairs to me. I fully expect you to oversee everything I do."

"Damn straight," he told her. "Not that I'm really thinkin' of taking you up on this insane offer of yours." But the truth of the matter was, that was exactly what he was thinking of doing. Part of him didn't trust her— or any woman—when it came to money. But he was down to no options. He was down to desperation.

"I still don't understand how you could delay the appraisal. You don't even work for the bank anymore."

"Technically, I still do. I got word of the layoff through my assistant. As of yet, I haven't been officially terminated. That means that I will have to go into the office on Monday morning."

"Not today?"

She pointed to her car. "How?"

"Right. Okay, so you go in Monday. And—"

"At this point I've made notes, but can't type the appraisal and put it into the system. Given the turmoil I expect to find in the office, even if they want me to finish the work, it would be simple to misfile it or put it into the wrong stack of papers. It would be days, maybe weeks before they found it, and chances are they would just reassign the appraisal, which would delay it even more. Of course, I can't guarantee that's what would happen, but almost."

When he continued to look dubious, she said, "This isn't as crazy as it sounds. I have no family. I'm an orphan, so you don't need to worry about a jealous husband or a father with a shotgun. I need—want to have a wild fling."

"Because?"

"Just...because."

"People don't go around deciding to have a wild fling every day of the week. You gotta have a reason."

"I want to, that's all."

"Because?"

"Why are you badgering me?"

"Because I want to know. And I'm not badgering you."

"Yes, you are."

"Just tell me."

"Because...I never had one, okay?" she snapped, feeling cornered. "Because I'm sick and tired of being a good girl and missing out on all the fun, okay? And because I want to see what it's like to give myself to passion, passion and more passion. Okay?"

"Okay," he said simply, apparently satisfied with her answer.

"I'm willing to trade my expertise in order to have what I want, and I'll give as good as I get. I have skills you need, and you have skills I... Well, let's just say I think it's an equitable trade."

"Skills?"

"Yes. And no money changes hands." Now that she'd finally spoken her piece she felt surprising calm. "And since this is strictly business, you don't have to worry that I'll want moonlight and roses. And I don't expect anything from you but—"

"Performance in bed."

"Well...yes."

"And what makes you think I'm qualified to take you on this wild ride you're looking for?"

"I, uh... Well, I understand you used to be a playboy of sorts."

"Cotton tell you that?"

She nodded.

"Yeah, well, he likes to brag."

Sam frowned. "So it's not true? You didn't go all those places...have all those women?"

He could end this nonsense right here, he realized. All he had to do was convince her she'd picked the wrong man. And he could do it. But he discovered he didn't want to. It might be perverse, but he wanted to see if she would really go through with it. "I've had my fair share. And with no complaints, I might add."

He could see the relief in her face and couldn't refrain from a little teasing. "Course, I'm usually the one doin' the chasin', so I'm not right sure how this would work. And there's always the possibility you might not like what you see. Or did you stop to think that we might get right down to it and I couldn't—"

"Has that ever happened to you before? I've heard of it happening to men, so if that's a concern—"

"No." Now it was his turn to frown. "Hell, no."

She smiled, reassured. "Then there's nothing to worry about. We'll use condoms, of course, so there'll be no concerns about protection."

"You've thought of everything, haven't you?"

"I hope so. You're healthy, right?"

"As a horse. You?"

"Absolutely."

Again, he leaned against the car and studied her. Of course he wasn't going to take her up on her offer. But she had guts, he'd give her that. He doubted she would go through with her plan, though. In fact, he had a surefire way to prove it.

The longer he stared at her the more nervous Sam got. "Are you thinking about—"

"I'm thinking that maybe we should do a test."

"A test?"

"Yeah, to see if we're even compatible. Sexually speaking."

Her eyes widened. "You mean...now?"

"Relax, Sam. I'm talking about a kiss." He couldn't help but grin at the startled look in her eyes. "Did you think I intended to toss you in the back seat of your car and jump you?"

"Well, I—"

"It's just a kiss," he said, moving slowly so not to startle her. He slipped his arms around her waist. "A simple little kiss."

But it was Ryder who wound up startled. And the kiss turned out to be anything but simple. He'd kissed a lot of woman in his time, but never had he felt such an instantaneous rush of heat. Before he could draw another breath he was hot clear through. Like being hit by lightning. Oh, yeah, definite electricity. Megawatts of it, in fact. And he couldn't swear the earth didn't move. Something was sure as hell trembling. It took him a couple of seconds to realize it was him. By that time he didn't care. He moved his tongue in and out of her mouth in a slow, hypnotic rhythm more to prolong his enjoyment than to arouse. More to savor her taste than satisfy the need spiraling through his body. His hands itched to touch her, stroke her everywhere. When his tongue met hers, she moaned, giving as good as she got. Then she sighed and melted against him. It was her sigh of acquiescence that finally tripped alarm bells in his head. Stunned and a little disoriented, he pulled back to look at her.

"Wow," Sam whispered.

"You can say that again."

"Well?" she asked, trying to calm her racing heart. "Did I pass?"

"With flying colors."

"So...?"

He took a deep breath and moved away just enough to get some air circulating between their bodies. Reason insisted this was all kinds of wrong, but his hormones weren't paying any attention. "I'm still thinking."

He was thinking, all right. About how long it had been since he'd been with a woman. About the two of them together, doing things she'd probably never dreamed of. About that needy little moan deep in her throat when he kissed her. It wasn't much of a leap to fantasize about her bucking beneath him in the throes of a wild climax. He was already hard.

And he was thinking about taking her up on her offer.

"Now, wait a minute," he said, as much for his benefit as hers. "My conscience won't let me do this." Neither would past lessons learned. How could he trust her? "I'd be taking advantage of you—"

"You wouldn't be."

"Yes," he insisted. "I would. No offense, but the chances of you being able to do anything effective to stop the foreclosure are damned slim, if not nonexistent." Saying the words out loud was like a knife in his heart.

"So, you're giving up on the ranch?"

Her words twisted the knife. "No," he insisted, ignoring the pain, focusing on determination. "Not until I've got no other choice. I told you I had some irons in the fire." True or not, he had to say it, had to convince himself the possibility of a miracle existed.

"You don't believe I can deliver."

"I want to believe it." He sighed. "You have no idea how much I want to believe—need to believe it."

"Then do." After a pause, she added, "I'm good at what I do, Ryder. I might not know much about..." She almost said men, but decided that was more information than he needed. "Flings, but I know how to handle numbers. I can't promise miracles, but the least I can do is buy you some extra time. As for the rest, you'll just have to take that on faith."

Faith. Something that had been in short supply around Copper Canyon lately. Yet here was a woman offering him just that. Old hurts and doubts gnawed at him. No, he couldn't give in, give up. He knew he was grasping at straws, but straws were all he had left. There were probably a dozen reasons for him not to take her deal. There was only one reason for him to say yes.

Hope.

She gave him hope. A light at the end of an otherwise dark tunnel, small though it might be. He couldn't turn his back on that hope.

The fact that he had so little to offer in return gave

him a moment of shame. Accepting was selfish, he knew, but the truth was he had nothing else. The hope that she might be able to help with the money was almost too fragile to hang on to, yet he found he was doing just that. If this worked, if, by some chance, this woman could pull off a miracle, he promised himself he would find a way to make it up to her. "When would you want to start this deal?"

Sam knew a moment of anxiety, then she squelched it. She'd made her decision and she intended to follow through. "How about tomorrow?"

"And exactly how had you planned to do this? Drive back and forth from your place to the ranch?"

She thought for a moment. "Now that you mention it, that wouldn't be very practical, would it?"

"Hardly."

"You've got empty cabins, don't you?"

"Yeah, and extra bedrooms in the house, or..."

"Or?

"There's a king-size bed in my room." They were down to the nitty-gritty. If she was going to change her mind, it would be now. The same went for him.

After another moment of consideration, she said, "I think the extra bedroom will do."

"Last chance to back out," Ryder told her.

"That goes both ways."

"You first."

Sam took a deep breath, mentally as well as physically. She wanted this. She could do this. In answer, she stepped close, pressed her body to his and kissed him. A second later she had to grab his shoulders to keep from crumpling into a heap. Her knees wouldn't support her, might never again. But what did knees matter when her toes were curling? What did anything matter when the world was exploding around her, in her? The only substantial thought she managed to process was that every cliché she'd ever heard or read about passionate kisses was absolutely true. The earth shifted beneath her feet. Fireworks shot and sparked around her. Her entire body felt on fire—a wonderful, ravenous fire. And how was it possible to feel as if her feet were rooted to the spot and her head was in the clouds at the same time? All the muscles in her body went limp. But not so limp she couldn't put her arms around his neck, pull him closer and deepen the kiss. Had she been as sober as she thought, the fact that they were standing where anyone who cared to look could see them would have shocked her, but it didn't. The only thing that registered was how much she wanted to touch him, run her fingers through his hair, slide her hands over the hard muscles of his chest. His bare chest. She moaned.

That little sound she made went through Ryder like a shot. He hadn't intended anything but an obligatory kiss, but that idea had gone to hell in a handbasket the minute her mouth had touched his. Operating on pure instinct, he slid his hand to the back of her head, angling her mouth under his to take complete possession. Satisfied he'd done just that, he slid one hand to the small of her back, the other to her hip, pressing her to him. Ryder forgot they were strangers, forgot who she was and why she was here. He forgot everything except the taste of her, the need to touch her. His hand slid up, stroked the soft fullness of her breast while he made love to her mouth. Even through the thin silk blouse he felt her nipples harden instantly. She clutched at the collar of his shirt, pressing herself against his hand. So responsive. So hot. So ready...

He ended the kiss out of sheer self-preservation for fear he just might go up in flames if he didn't.

"You got yourself a deal," he said, and hoped he didn't self-combust before she worked her numbers miracle.

3

"WHERE THE HELL'S your truck?" Cotton said as he came through the back door into the kitchen bright and early the next morning.

Ryder was at the counter pouring himself a cup of coffee. "I loaned it to Miss Collins. Sam. She's, uh, bringing it back today, and she'll be staying here for a while."

"You gone plumb loco?"

"Possibly," Ryder mumbled.

"Jest cause she ain't got a job is no reason to take her in like a lost puppy."

"I'm not. She's got a background in business management and she's got some money contacts. For the next week or so she'll be here day and night, checking everything out, making recommendations to streamline—"

"Day and night?"

"You heard me."

Cotton grinned, then the grin turned up into a full smile, and he chuckled. "I get it. Well, if that's the story you wanna tell, fine by me. And don't worry. I'll make sure Mamie don't go waggin' her tongue."

"Now listen, Cotton..." Ryder stopped himself, deciding maybe it was better to let Cotton think Sam's presence meant a romance. It's what everyone would think, regardless of the truth.

"What?" Cotton asked.

"Don't...go overboard, okay? Just because a woman is staying here for a while doesn't make it the romance of the century, all right?"

"Shore, but you gotta admit it's a first. And 'bout time, if you ask me."

"Okay. Just don't get crazy on me, and start making more of it."

Cotton shook his finger, gave him a knowing wink. "I knew you was interested the way you looked her up and down right off the bat. I got to go tell Mamie."

"Tell Mamie what?" his wife said, coming through the back door.

"Ryder's got hisself a girl."

"You don't mean it."

"It's that lady banker. And she's gonna be stayin' here."

Mamie turned to Ryder. "That a fact?"

"It's a fact."

"Well—" Mamie put her hands on her ample hips "—it's about damn time."

"'Xactly what I told him."

Ryder looked at the two people who were like family and felt a twinge of guilt. He knew they cared about him and wanted him to be happily married and settled. But this wasn't it, and he hated to burst their bubble. "It's only temporary, guy. Don't get any ideas, okay?"

They both agreed, but he didn't care for the gleam in Mamie's eyes.

"When's she comin'?" she asked.

"This afternoon."

By the afternoon Ryder admitted he was a little nervous. He half expected Sam to call saying she'd changed her mind and he should come get his truck. As the day progressed, that thought grew until finally he realized just how disappointed he'd be if that call came. Leaning against the corral railing, he looked down the empty road. He was looking forward to tonight. To more kisses and beyond.

Kissing a woman was just about his favorite pastime, and he'd always considered it his duty as a gentleman and potential lover to make kisses, especially first kisses, as pleasurable as the law allowed. Over the years he'd honed his skills to a sweet expertise, always the one in control because that's the way he liked it. Old hurts notwithstanding, he still did.

But he'd lost control of kissing Sam almost from the moment their lips touched.

She might not have known it, in fact he was positive she hadn't, but he knew it. And it worried him. He told himself his powerful reaction was due to the fact that he hadn't been with a woman in a while. And that the ranch had taken up all his time and energy. But whatever reason he used, he admitted to feeling a little...unsteady about how to approach consummating their deal. And that he didn't like. Unsteadiness wasn't in his vocabulary. Hell, he'd parachuted from planes, raced over treacherous roads, jumped out of high-rise buildings and performed a million other stunts. Making love had about as much risk as falling off a log. He heard his truck approaching and breathed a sigh of relief. He was beside the truck before she even killed the motor.

"Need some help?" he asked, opening the door for her.

"I've just got one suitcase." She turned off the engine, grabbed her purse and a shopping bag.

"For a week? I've seen women come in here with ten times this much for a two-night stay."

"I travel light." She didn't want him to know she'd spent most of the morning trying to decide what clothes to bring, the afternoon giving herself a manicure, pedicure and conditioning her hair. And she certainly didn't want him to know she'd stopped at Stonebriar Mall on her way back to buy bath oil, body lotion and a new fragrance, then detoured into Victoria's Secret. Considering she was unemployed, the money she'd spent wasn't trivial, but she considered it a necessary expense. And a guilty pleasure. Although she had a passion for scented lotions and body oils, she'd never indulged in such deliciously sensual lingerie in her life. She had to admit it felt extravagantly naughty, but good. And for her time with Ryder it was important to have new things to go with the new direction of her life.

"Sugar, if those jeans are a sample, I'd say you made great selections."

Sam smiled. She'd changed into a T-shirt and her favorite pair of jeans. They were relaxed enough to be comfortable, but tight enough to enhance her fanny and emphasize her legs. "Thank you."

He reached around her, plucked the medium-size suitcase from the seat and caught the subtle fragrance of her perfume, light and alluring. When he closed the door she was standing just close enough for him to lean in, breathe deep, his face inches from hers. "You smell great." He drew back, his killer blue eyes intense. "Ready?"

She knew the question had a double meaning. Lord knew, she'd asked herself the same thing at least a dozen times during the past hours. But despite the fact that she admitted to a reasonable amount of fear, the answer had always been the same, an unqualified yes. "Absolutely," she said, her voice clear, strong and free of hesitation as he led her inside.

The kitchen was filled with the most delicious aroma.

"I wasn't sure exactly when you'd be back, so Mamie fixed some fried chicken and potato salad." There was a knock at the back door. "I'm not surprised," Ryder said, rolling his eyes.

"Who is it?"

"Unless I'm wrong, a couple of well-meaning busybodies." He opened the door to find Cotton and Mamie. "C'mon in."

"I figured you'd want some apple pie to go with that chicken." Mamie spoke to Ryder, but her attention was on Sam.

"Nothin' like hot apple pie," Cotton said.

"Or nosy friends."

"Jest wanted to say a proper welcome. By the by," Mamie told Sam, "sorry 'bout yesterday."

"Excuse me?"

"You know. Thinkin' you and Cotton—"

"That's perfectly all right. And I can understand how you want to keep a close eye on a man like Cotton," Sam teased.

"Well, he ain't much, but he's mine."

"Talkin' like I was some prize bull," Cotton huffed. But Sam noticed a blush creep over his cheeks.

"Thanks for the pie," Ryder said. "I know y'all like to turn in early, so we won't keep you."

Cotton winked at his wife. "Think that's a hint?"

"He never was very subtle, was he?"

A moment later Ryder and Sam were again alone.

"They're nice people," Sam said.

"They're nosy as hell but the closest thing to family that I've got. And I have to admit Mamie makes the best apple pie in the county. Are you hungry?"

Her hand automatically went to her stomach, but it was more to quiet the nerves dancing inside and the trembling of her hands. "Not very."

"Well, then, I'll show you the guest room."

The bedroom was small but tidy and slightly feminine with faded cabbage rose wallpaper. The quilt on the antique tester bed looked the same age as the wallpaper and was hand-stitched. Not exactly the uncluttered modern style she was accustomed to. In fact, she usually avoided obviously feminine florals and ruffles, but she found the room oddly comforting. She wondered if this room had once belonged to his mother or grandmother.

"Make yourself at home," Ryder said from the doorway. "I'm gonna catch a quick shower. Afterward, if you've changed your mind, we can eat. If not, maybe a walk down by the pond. We got a hell of a sunset working."

"We don't have to."

"What?"

"You don't have to take me for a walk at sunset," she told him. "I was serious when I said I didn't require moonlight and roses."

He looked at her standing there, all soft curves and need, her pulse beating in her throat like a hummingbird's wings, her hands shaking. *Poor baby*, he thought. *Her last lover must have been a real jerk.*

"I mean, I just don't want you to think it's necessary to—"

"It isn't necessary." He walked to her, slipped a hand beneath her hair and caressed the back of her neck. "It's a pleasure. And tonight's all about pleasure."

His touch, his promise, made her shiver, tingle and want everything the word *pleasure* implied. "Oh."

"Relax," he said, letting his hands skim down her shoulders to her elbows in a casual caress before he stepped away. "I'll be back in a minute."

Minute? An hour wouldn't be a sufficient amount of time to stop the trembling that seemed to have taken complete control of her body. One touch and she was weak in the knees. God only knew what would happen when they had their clothes off. Sam closed her eyes, sighing in sweet anticipation mixed with almost equal amounts of trepidation. Suddenly, her inexperience loomed large. *Tonight's all about pleasure,* he had promised. Exactly what she wanted, what she'd bargained for, wasn't it? Yes, she thought, a feeling of courage beginning to make her feel more relaxed. Yes, this was what she wanted.

When he walked out of his bathroom into his bedroom he heard Sam humming. Obviously, she'd taken his advice and relaxed. He smiled, feeling a little like humming himself. Fifteen minutes later he closed the door to his bedroom, strolled down the hall. As he knocked on the guest room door it swung open. "I thought we'd..."

Whatever thought had been in his brain vanished completely. She was standing by the window, the last rays of the day shimmering gold against her skin and wearing nothing but a pale turquoise nightgown. The reason he knew she had nothing else on was that the gown had a slit on one side from her ankle almost to her waist, exposing a long bare leg and hip. And the neckline dipped almost to her navel, giving him a mind-boggling view of her barely lace-covered breasts and leaving almost nothing to the imagination. He couldn't do anything but stare.

While Sam had waited for him she'd banished her last bit of nerves and given her imagination free rein, letting the anticipation build, race through her body. She deliberately stepped away from the window and came toward him. "I decided there would be another sunset tomorrow. You're not disappointed, are you?"

Ryder's heart slammed against his rib cage like he'd just parachuted out of a plane with twenty cameras rolling for a million-dollar shot. His breath came unevenly. Finally he found his voice and enough air in his lungs to make it work. "Sugar, I'm a lot of things right now, but disappointed is definitely not one of them."

Smiling, she came closer. "That's good." If she'd thought he was handsome this afternoon under a glaring sun, he was devastating now, his hair slightly damp from his shower, his shoulders so broad they practically filled the doorway. And his blue eyes, dark as a midnight sky, his gaze so intense, so hot, she could almost feel the heat. She'd been right about him. He was born to make women forget about everything but this man.

"I thought there were some things about me you should know."

"Such as?"

"I don't tease and I don't pretend."

Ryder smiled. "I figured that out yesterday."

She smiled. "I guess that holds true for both of us. I just meant—"

"I know what you meant."

Anyone who overheard their conversation might have assumed they were discussing character traits, but they knew differently. This conversation was on a single track and leading straight to sex. No skirting the subject.

"That's good." She came closer until she was directly in front of him, close enough so all she need do was lean a few inches and her breasts would touch his chest. And she wanted to do that. Ached to do that. "Know what I remember most about last night?" Without waiting for an answer she said, "Kissing you. And I was thinking—fantasizing actually—about how it would be even better tonight."

"That makes two of us."

Then, in spite of the last little pang of nerves, she did what she'd longed to do. She leaned toward him until their bodies touched. "Kiss me, Ryder."

It was a personally delivered, heat-stamped invitation he eagerly accepted, but with his own style of RSVP. As much as he wanted to yank her to him and devour her mouth, he didn't. God knows where he got the strength to resist the urge, but he reached out and traced her mouth with the tip of his finger. Once. Twice. He heard her breath catch, felt her shudder and her nipples harden. He caressed her neck as he'd done earlier, then slowly, still not embracing her, he leaned in and kissed first one corner of her mouth then the other. With his other hand he tilted her head, giving him access to her neck, and he took full advantage, kissing the delicate skin along her jaw, down her throat to the pulse point beating wildly. And he kept going, lifting her hair to taste the nape of her neck. All the while kissing her, savoring the sweet taste of her.

His mouth was so hot against her skin and getting hotter with every breath. Every inch of her body tingled, vibrating with need as he pushed the strap of the nightgown from her shoulder, then placed random kisses from that spot to her earlobe and back, then over her collarbone. She clutched at his shirt, trying to bring him closer, needing him closer. "Ryder," she sighed. "Kiss me."

His answer was to trail soft, seductive kisses over the inviting swell of her breasts. And when he ran his tongue along the lacy edge of the gown's daring bodice, she whimpered. "Kiss me."

But this time she didn't wait for an answer, taking matters, and his face, into her own hands. At her touch he lifted his head and met her gaze. The intensity in his eyes was scorching. Thrilling. Demanding. Exciting. Everything in her responded. She wanted the thrill, the demand, the excitement. She wanted it the same way she wanted him. Totally. Completely.

"Now," she demanded. "Kiss me now."

A tiny, triumphant smile tilted the corner of his mouth as he acceded to her urgent demand. He yanked her into his arms as his mouth took total, inexorable possession of hers. He kissed her long, hard, taking all she would give, stoking the hunger. He feasted on her mouth, taking the kiss deeper. Somewhere in the back of his mind he remembered a vague intent to take her slow and gentle this first time, but it was no good. Had been no good from the instant he saw her standing against the sunset, ready, waiting. Next time, he promised himself. If he lived that long.

Sam went on her tiptoes, wrapped her arms around his neck, arching her spine to bring him as close as possible. It wasn't enough. She wanted, needed to be closer. *Had* to have him closer. She slid her hands down his back to his taut, narrow hips, slipping her hands into his back pockets to pull him to her. She rotated her hips against his erection and moaned.

He decided that sound would probably kill him, but he didn't care. Still kissing her, Ryder put his hands on her hips and guided her toward the bed until he felt her legs make contact. Only then did he stop kissing her long enough to pull the remaining strap down, tugging the gown to her waist.

She was flawless. Perfect. When he took her breasts in his big callused hands they filled his palms, soft and ripe, the nipples dark red against her smooth, creamy skin. He cupped both breasts, rubbing his thumbs back and forth over her nipples.

"Oh," she gasped.

"Did I hurt you?"

"No!" She put her hands over his, encouraged his caresses. "It just feels so...so—" she took a deep, shuddering breath "—good."

Ryder grinned. "Hang on, sugar. It's gonna feel a lot better."

"Promise?"

"Oh, yeah. And I never make promises I can't keep."

He was right—it got better. So much better Sam wasn't sure she could stand it. But not only did she stand it, she begged for more. Ryder gladly complied. His hands were everywhere and magic. His mouth... Oh, his wonderful, inquisitive, seductive, hot mouth. His lips branding her everywhere they touched. And they touched her everywhere. In places she'd never realized were so sensitive, so responsive. The corner of her mouth. Just her bottom lip. The sweet spot in the valley of her breasts, perfect for his tongue. The curve of her waist seconds after he pushed the gown over her hips and it fell to the floor. And the tender area just below her navel where he planted soft, hungry, openmouthed kisses that made her quiver. Made her moan.

"No...no fair," she whispered, her voice raspy with a need so strong it almost took her breath away.

"What?" He nibbled at her ear, her neck.

"You have...have on...too many clothes."

"Not a problem." He all but ripped his shirt off. Before he could finish removing his jeans, she reached for him. She kissed his mouth, then she moved to his neck, his shoulder and took tiny nips at his flesh. The more she touched him, tasted him, the more aggressive she became. Driven by a primeval need that threatened her sanity, she couldn't stop.

Ryder struggled with the resistant denim, nearly driven wild to be free, crazy to be skin to skin. As he kicked free of the jeans and pushed her down on the bed, he kissed her like he was already inside her. Hard and deep.

She held her breath, waiting, craving for him to fill her body the way he'd filled her mouth. Instead, he seemed to take a deep breath, slow down. His hands wandered over her, starting at her shoulders then over her breasts, hips and thighs. He stroked, caressed all the way to her ankles, then along the inside of her thighs. Like an explorer he mapped her body, familiarizing himself with every inch of her. The turn of her hips, the slope of her breasts, the flat plain of her tummy. All of her, until she whimpered, clutching the bedsheet, her body twisting, needing.

"Please, oh, please."

But he wasn't ready to give her everything all at once. Where he found the strength and control, he wasn't sure. All he knew was that once he was inside her there would be no more strength, no more control, only hot, deep and endless pleasure. Barely able to hold out, he cupped her heated core then slipped a finger into the moist, swollen folds of flesh between her legs.

She thrust her hips upward and cried out as the first climax rolled through her. "Oh, please, please, Ryder. I want you...want you inside me..."

"Almost, sugar. Just a little more."

"More," she repeated, mindless with desire, and got her wish.

He slid two fingers into her, rotating his thumb against her nub, withdrew, then repeated the motion, kept repeating the motion until she writhed against his hand. She climaxed again, a shuddering, trembling release. She reached for him only to have him pull away, roll to the side of the bed.

She moaned. "Don't—"

"Protection, sugar." He opened a drawer of the bedside table, took out a foil-wrapped packet, ripped it open and sheathed his erection. "You're so hot." He moved to her. "You make me so crazy it nearly slipped my mind." This time when she reached for him, he was there. He lay over her, slid both hands beneath her hips, then buried himself in her to the hilt.

And then the world turned upside down and shook. He pounded into her, hard, deep, relentless. She thrust her hips up to meet him, pumping wildly, until finally completion lashed through her like lightning.

With each stroke, Ryder's control slipped. He tried to hang on, tried to stay in control, but it was useless. He was lost, unable to do anything but drive toward completion, toward pleasure so intense he thought he might explode. And then he did, gloriously, endlessly, spilling into her.

What felt like a long time later Ryder roused himself and pulled the covers over them. She stirred, curling into him like a sleeping kitten. Unable to resist, he lightly ran his hand over the sleek curve of her hip, down her thigh.

"Mmm, that feels wonderful." She stretched, unfolding her body in a tempting arch then scooted closer, slipping her slender leg over his hard, muscled thigh. "Don't stop."

Stop touching her? Stop wanting her? He wasn't sure he could do either. "Your skin is so incredibly soft," he said, continuing to caress her, touch her. He palmed her breast, savoring the fullness, the delicate texture of her flesh. "So soft."

She sighed, her hips instinctively rotating against his leg. "I'd like to credit my genes but since I'm not sure of their origin, I'll have to admit to a passion for lotions and bath oils."

He brushed a mass of strawberry blond curls from her shoulder, kissed it. "There's not a bath oil on the market that can produce skin like this." He linked his fingers with hers, brought her hand to his lips, turned it and kissed the inside of her wrist. "And I don't taste a trace of lotion. I taste you. Sweet, salty—" he licked the tip of her index finger "—sexy."

Her body already humming with need, she raised up on one elbow, leaned forward and touched her tongue to his nipple. "And you taste—" she looked at him "—hot. Hard."

Taking full advantage of her inviting position, he reached between their bodies and found her dewy, swollen flesh ready for his nimble fingers. She closed her eyes, let her head fall back and rocked against his hand, giving herself over to need, to him.

"Don't know about hot, but you've got the hard part right." He slipped on a condom and in one quick stroke planted himself inside her.

She gasped. Her eyes flew open, sparking with fire. With a cry she clutched his shoulder and started to move. Shifting her hips, she met him stroke for stroke, giving as good as she got. Panting, shuddering, all she could think was *more*.

Unable to get enough of her, he spread his hand over her butt, his fingertips almost digging into her flesh, and plunged deeper, faster. She arched, taking all of him, welcoming the unrelenting, surging power. Higher, hotter and faster they went until they were sucked into a fierce, white-hot vortex, totally consumed then flung up, out and into a shimmering void together.

SAM WOKE UP to bright sunlight and the sound of Ryder humming as he walked down the hall toward the kitchen. Like the consummate satisfied feline she stretched long and lazy, savoring the last glow of pleasure. She decided there wasn't a muscle she hadn't used, a patch of skin that didn't tingle. Her mouth—she ran her tongue over her lips—was still swollen from Ryder's kisses. And the truth was, if he walked into the room this minute she would want him as much as she had last night. She'd never felt so deliciously naughty, so gloriously satisfied, in her life. This, she could get used to. This, she could get addicted to. Sex had never, ever been so consuming, so obsessive, so... There weren't enough words to describe it, or how she felt. The only thing she knew for certain was that she felt whole, complete and more connected to Ryder than she had to any person in her life. They had a deal, though, not a romance, and she wasn't sure that was good, but there wasn't anything she could do about it. It simply was. Besides, too much time spent analyzing what had happened last night, or her feelings, defeated her purpose. She should get on with the day.

Sam threw back the covers, swung her legs over the edge of the bed and glanced at her body. She'd never slept naked in her life, not even with a lover. At the first twinge of guilt born out of years of lectures, she closed that door in her mind, locked it. The sisters at the orphanage would have been appalled, but the truth was she'd enjoyed every second of her time with Ryder. Loved every second. Confidence surged through her. Yes, she had to get on with the day.

So she could get to the night.

By the time she'd showered, dressed in jeans and a T-shirt and made it to the kitchen, Ryder was settled at the table drinking coffee.

"Good morning," he said mildly, barely looking up.

"Morning." Sam wanted to walked across the floor, wrap her arms around him and kiss him, but she decided against it. From the cool shoulder he was giving her she didn't think he'd appreciate it. After all, they did have a deal. "You should have woken me."

"Didn't have the heart. You were sleeping so soundly."

"Hmm."

She sighed, and he felt his blood quicken. This wouldn't do, or every time they were in the same room he'd have to fight the urge to rip her clothes off and take her again. As soon as she'd walked into the kitchen, he'd wanted to sweep her up and back into the bedroom. He'd only been able to stop himself by avoiding looking into her sexy, sleep-softened face. He wasn't quite sure what she wanted out of this deal and didn't want to scare her off. "Coffee?" He pointed to an empty cup on the counter.

"Thanks. Maybe I'll set the alarm tomorrow morning."

"That'll work."

Sam poured herself a cup of coffee, debating whether or not she should follow his lead, act as if nothing had happened between them, or go with her usual forthright nature. Nature won. Cup in hand, she turned to him.

"So, we're not going to talk about it?"

"It?"

"Last night. You, me and the hottest sex on the planet."

He smiled for the first time. "I was waiting to see your reaction. You said strictly business, so I figured you might just want to put it out of your mind, concentrate on today."

"Can *you* do that?"

"I'd have to be dead to be able to put last night out of my mind."

She smiled, walked to him. "But you may have a point about concentrating."

"Yeah?"

"To be honest, I can't promise that what we did to, and for, each other won't stroll into my thoughts as the day progresses, but I think I can manage to get some work done." She ran her hand up his arm, felt the muscles beneath her fingers tense. "Of course, I've got my work cut out for me to equal your end of the deal."

Still grinning, he winked. "Thank you, ma'am. We aim to please."

"Trust me. It was a bull's-eye."

"You know, I don't think you told me the truth yesterday. You do tease."

"Only when it's harmless—"

A knock on the back door intruded. "Mornin'," Mamie said, coming through the door a second later. "Y'all hungry?"

"Starved," Sam replied, deciding it was a good thing Mamie had opened that door and walked in. The air in the kitchen was already a little too warm for comfort.

After breakfast Ryder took Sam into his office and showed her the files, the billing system and the computer setup.

"I need to spend a few minutes going over some stuff with Cotton. If you need anything, just sing out. Mamie knows where most everything is, but I won't be long."

"All right."

Ryder walked outside, breathed deeply, then stuffed his hands into his pockets while he waited. And thought about Sam.

He didn't get it. For the life of him he didn't understand how a woman like Sam was still walking around loose. She was...*mind-blowing* was the only word he could find. This utterly gorgeous, mind-blowing woman had shown up on his doorstep and asked for sex. He didn't get it. Were all the men in Dallas too busy or too stupid not to recognize a diamond when it was right under their noses? All he could say was their loss was absolutely, positively his gain. Last night had been one of the most amazing nights of his life. Totally amazing. Ryder closed his eyes, savoring the memory. God, how he'd missed feeling that close...

His eyes flew open. Yeah, he'd missed the kind of closeness only a man and a woman could share. And he'd missed waking up to the touch and the taste of a warm, willing woman. But he hadn't forgotten that there was a price for all that closeness. And he wasn't so sure he was ready to ante up. If he wasn't careful he could end up on the short end of the stick again. While his intellect and his instincts told him Sam wasn't anything like Alicia, his heart wasn't so sure. He'd been deceived once, and as much as he hated to admit it, he could be again. Sam was one hot number, but he wasn't in a hurry to get burned a second time.

Satisfied that he was once again firmly rooted in reality, Ryder walked to the barn and found Cotton inside. After a short discussion on the day's schedule, he went to the house to see how Sam was doing.

"Who keeps your books?" she asked the instant he walked through the door.

"You're lookin' at him."

She thought for a moment. "Please don't be offended when I say that may need to be the first thing we change."

"I'm not offended. But why? I'm cheap labor."

"Yes, but it probably takes up a great deal of your time."

"Too damn much. Probably because I hate it and drag my feet."

"Exactly. I know this sounds like I'm asking you to spend money when we're trying to save it, but your time and talents are better utilized on the ranch, not in the office. I know you don't want to hand the entire business workings over to someone else, but a bookkeeper's salary would be worth the hassle factor alone. Plus, it would free you up for more hands-on time with potential clients, which would mean more money. You're much more valuable as a marketing tool then you are as a bean counter."

"Never thought of it like that."

"The next step is to review employee time sheets,

utility bills. Oh, and I'd like to see a list of your suppliers," she said, furiously making notes as she talked.

"Any particular reason?"

"Chances are you've been using most of them for a long time, right?"

"Most."

"And there's nothing wrong with that. But there's a possibility that with a little research we could find new ones. With good customer service recommendations," she was quick to add. "And, more important, willing to beat your current costs."

"A few of our vendors have been doing business with Copper Canyon Ranch since my dad was running the place. They're friends."

They'd hit the first pothole on the road to a successful, viable business. How Ryder dealt with it would determine how much help he was truly willing to accept. "Are their businesses a hobby?"

"Well, no."

"Neither is yours." She looked him straight in the eyes. "Ryder, I can only provide you with information and recommendations. You're not obligated to take anything I say and run with it."

"But?"

"But you have to be willing to look at your situation more objectively than you have before, and willing to implement some changes, or you might as well call your lawyer right now for some advice about bankruptcy. It's as simple as that."

"You're right." It dawned on him just how right she was. She'd hit on simple things, but simple or not, he'd never thought of them. "And I am willing. Guess I got my back up for a minute. It won't happen again."

"Oh, yes, it will. But I promise it's not fatal. And if it makes you feel any better, no matter what new sources I find, your current vendors should have an opportunity to meet whatever new bids are offered. You just have to keep reminding yourself that this is business. The good old boys may be great as friends, but they're not paying your bills."

"I get your drift."

"Of course, there's another avenue we could explore in addition to reorganization, and that's an infusion of capital."

"You mean another loan?"

"Not necessarily. I was thinking more along the lines of an investor. Someone willing to—"

"A partner?"

"Well, possibly."

"Forget it," he said flatly.

"But why? As long as you can be assured the person is honest and you retain controlling interest—"

"That's just it. Partners are a risk. Can't count on them staying honest even if they start out that way. And controlling interest don't mean squat if they decide to clean you out." He shook his head. "Can't trust 'em. I'd go down in flames before I took on a partner."

Clearly, this was a real issue with him. His voice, body language, even the way his eyes darkened, told her it was not only an issue, but a touchy one. "Since you obviously have trust issues, I take it you've had a bad experience with a partner."

"Damn straight. We probably wouldn't be having this conversation—in fact, you'd probably never have had a reason to come here at all—if I hadn't trusted a—" he took a deep breath "—partner."

"You had a partner in the ranch?"

"No. When I was in California." After a moment he said, "A woman." Then another pause before he added, "And I'm sure Cotton filled you in on the rest."

"Not the details," she admitted.

"Well, Alicia was clever enough to make sure she was always the one to deal with my agent, convincing me to take the high-risk, high-dollar jobs. She said it was good for my career. The bigger the stunts, the bigger my name in the business. I didn't know she was not only taking credit for managing my career and skimming the profits, but sleeping with someone else as well, until it was too late."

"No wonder you weren't comfortable with the idea of a woman handling any part of your business. I'm sorry, Ryder."

"Yeah, well..." He rose from the chair next to hers and paced the length of the office a couple of times as if he were trying to walk off the memory. She waited for him to speak. "So, do me a favor and forget about a partner for Copper Canyon, okay?"

"Okay," she said, and decided to change the subject. "Why don't you tell me about whatever software you use for the day-to-day operations."

Eventually, the tension eased, and they worked steadily for the next three hours, mostly collecting the information Sam needed to review. The more she talked, the more she explained how he could reorganize and maximize his current situation, the more she saw her esteem rating rise. His opinion of her abilities had obviously increased immeasurably. She wasn't offended. In fact, she'd expected him to have doubts. But she did need him to have confidence in her for any of her ideas to work.

They broke for lunch—tuna sandwiches, fruit and Mamie's homemade potato chips. Sam noticed that, as she had at breakfast, Mamie cooked, cleaned up, then made herself scarce, and she wondered if that was the norm or because there was a guest in the house. She didn't want to upset whatever routine existed before she arrived, but she also had to admit that she liked the feeling of just her and Ryder alone in the house. After lunch Sam went back to her review of vendors and time sheets. Ryder went to make sure everything was in order for the small corporate party the following day. She took a short break for a glass of iced tea around three o'clock, but felt as if she were fighting an uphill battle in a sea of paperwork by the time she heard Mamie coming in the back door.

"Hey, there," Mamie said when Sam walked into the kitchen. Several grocery sacks sat on the counter along with a case of beer.

"For the party tomorrow?" Sam asked.

"Heavens, no. It's for tonight. I gotta bake a chocolate cake or there'll be hell to pay. Normally, I'd tote this stuff over to the big kitchen, but the meat truck just arrived, and I'd be under foot for sure."

"What's going on tonight? Another function?"

Mamie laughed. "If you call men, beer, cards and poker chips a function."

"I don't understand."

"It's Saturday night, honey. Time for the regular poker game."

"Poker?"

"Sure. Along 'bout dark a bunch them heathen cowboys'll congregate over to the big hall and play till they drop or go broke, whichever comes first. It's what goes on at Copper Canyon on Saturday night. Guess it musta slipped Ryder's mind."

"Yes. I guess it must have."

"Actually, it's just penny ante stuff. Ryder wouldn't stand still for a body losin' his shirt. But my, oh, my, they crank up the jukebox and have themselves a high old time, I'll tell you."

Sam grinned. "I would have thought the men might go into town where they could find some livelier entertainment, not to mention ladies."

"Oh, now, they do their fair share of carousin', that's for sure. But Ryder's dad fixed up these games years ago 'cause he got tired of losin' hands to boozin' and brawlin'. Come Sunday mornin' like as not he'd haveta bail a coupla hands outta jail so they could work."

"I see."

Mamie saw the expression on her face and read it right. "Oh, now, don't you go gettin' down in the mouth thinkin' your man'd rather be with a buncha hairy-legged old cowboys than with you. Why, I wouldn't be surprised if he don't last but a coupla hands 'fore he beats a path right back to the house."

She sidled up to Sam and in a lowered voice said, "Jest between you, me and the gate post I been plumb worried about Ryder's, uh, well-bein', you might say. Ain't healthy for a man to go too long without a woman—the right woman—to make him feel like a man, if you get my drift."

"Yes, I think I do," Sam told her, squelching a smile when she realized Mamie was serious.

"Now, I know my opinion ain't very, whaddaya-callit, politically correct. But it's sure as hell worked jest fine for me and that old fool I married. Goin' on forty-five years now." She crossed her arms over her chest, nodded. "You know what they say. If it ain't broke, don't fix it."

"Sound advice."

Mamie looked at her as if trying to decide if Sam was just being polite. "Oh, listen to me spoutin' off," she said. "Your mama probably give you the same advice when you was a girl."

"Actually—" Sam glanced away "—I never knew my mother. I grew up in a Catholic orphanage."

"Well, bless your heart, honey."

"And I'm afraid the advice I received about men wasn't nearly as plain or colorful. I like your version better."

The compliment brought a wide grin from the older woman. "I knew I liked you right off the bat. Say, how'd you like to help me make that cake?"

"I'm not much of a cook, but I'm a quick study. I'm game if you are."

WHEN RYDER RETURNED he found them in the kitchen. Sam had flour up to her elbows, across her forehead and down the front of her shirt. Mamie was only marginally cleaner. And they were both laughing like they'd been friends for years.

"You ladies been nippin' at the cooking sherry?" he asked.

Sam whirled around at the sound of his voice, breathless from laughter—and the sight of him didn't help. When he crooked a finger at her, her heart nearly stopped.

"C'mere," he said. When she walked to him he brushed a smear of cocoa from her cheek and thought how cute she looked, all bright-eyed and breathless from laughing. And sexy. Always sexy. "There's something I forgot to tell you about—"

"The poker game? Mamie told me."

"And that ain't all I told," Mamie teased, sliding two cake pans filled with batter into the oven before leaving the room—and leaving them alone.

"I don't think I want to know," Ryder said, watching Mamie's exit. Then he returned his gaze to Sam. "I'm sorry I didn't tell you this mornin', but—"

"That's all right. We both had other things on our mind."

Ryder stared at her mouth, wanting to kiss her. Wanting to do a lot more than settle for just a kiss. Timing, he reminded himself, was everything. "Tell you what. I'll cancel the game for tonight."

"You will not. The men look forward to these games.

It's their recreation, and it wouldn't be fair for you to cancel."

"Mamie *has* been talkin', hasn't she?"

"Besides which, I've never seen a poker game. Can I watch?"

"Don't know how well I'll be able to concentrate with you in the room, but you can watch if you want to."

"But you do play, and you can teach me, right?"

"Damn straight."

"Good. Although, I don't expect that it will be difficult. It's just a matter of keeping track of the numbers. As you know, I'm very good with numbers. And I insist we play for real."

She was like a double shot of hard liquor, straight to the brain. He couldn't resist being this close and not touching her, so he put a hand on her hip and brought her closer. "Anytime, sugar. I'd just love to take your money."

She toyed with the snap on his Western shirt. "I wasn't thinking about using money."

"Matchsticks?"

"Guess I didn't make myself clear." She pressed her hip against his leg and was pleased when she felt him tense in response. "Ryder, I want you to teach me how to play strip poker."

4

MAMIE INSISTED they all have dinner together before the poker game, so the four of them shared leftover fried chicken to which she had added macaroni salad and corn on the cob fresh from her garden. They laughed, teased, with Mamie and Cotton telling stories about Ryder as a child. It was a "Leave It to Beaver" kind of meal. The kind Sam had dreamed about as a kid. Ryder, Cotton and Mamie had formed a makeshift family, accepted it as the ordinary and couldn't possibly know what an extraordinary treasure a simple family meal was. And even though she'd only known them a little more than twenty-four hours, she felt welcomed.

Sam hated for it to end. And not just because she liked Mamie and Cotton and enjoyed their company. She was slightly apprehensive about joining the poker game, something that according to Mamie was a Copper Canyon tradition. It was a little like being taken home to meet your boyfriend's family, though of course Ryder wasn't a real boyfriend. But what if the men thought she was intruding or just didn't like her? Would that influence Ryder enough to cancel their deal?

By the time they arrived at the dining hall, the beer

was cold, the jukebox was playing Trisha Yearwood and the game was noisy, and in full swing. At least six of the ranch's ten hands were present, including one man with his wife and two kids. Mamie waved to the woman sitting with the kids in front of a big screen television at the other end of the room.

"'Bout time y'all showed up," one of the hands called.

"You in such an all-fired hurry to part with yore money?" Cotton asked, finding a place at the round table that easily seated ten.

"In a hurry to take yours," the cowboy replied, and they all laughed.

Ryder pointed to the man dealing the cards. "They're playing Texas Hold 'Em," he told Sam.

"Is that a kind of poker?"

One of the men overheard her question. "The only kind worth playin'," he announced.

"Outside of five-card stud." Another chimed in.

"Hey, boss, how come you're not sittin' in?" the dealer asked.

"I'll get around to it, but right now I'm telling Miss Collins how the game's played." Casually, he slipped an arm around her waist.

One of the men got up from the table. "Whatcha wanna go and do that for? Just be somebody else to beat ya. You won't have to learn too much, miss," the man said as he walked past them to the beer cooler. "He's a lousy poker player."

"Remind me to dock you," Ryder quipped.

"Hey, no sweat. With you playin' I'll make it up in one hand."

"Maybe I should get him to teach me," Sam teased.

Ryder shot a warning look at the cowboy. "Over my dead body. Now, like I was saying before I was interrupted," Ryder went on, "Texas Hold 'Em uses forced bets. The player to the dealer's left has to kick in, and so does the man next to him."

"Forced?"

"Means they have to bet even before the cards are dealt."

"Why would they do that if they don't even know what cards they'll get?"

"I don't make the rules, sugar. I'm just explaining them."

"In other words, you don't know."

Cotton piped up. "You got that right."

Somebody else added, "Amen."

"Why don't y'all just shut up and tend to your cards," Ryder told them.

The lesson in Texas Hold 'Em went downhill from there with Ryder trying his best to show her the finer points and his employees taking potshots at his efforts. But it was all good-natured ribbing. And the best part as far as Sam was concerned was that Ryder kept her close to him. The entire time he was talking he held her hand, put his arm around her waist or draped it over her shoulder. By the time a young cowboy named Scooter gave Ryder his seat, she was much less interested in poker. Just being with Ryder was enough. He continued to instruct as he played, but with the additional teasing comments, it became increasingly complex. Normally fascinated by anything numerical, she decided not to fight the confusion and wait for a private lesson. When she glanced over and saw Mamie bring out the chocolate cake, it was with relief to lightly tap Ryder on the arm and say, "Think I'll help Mamie, okay?"

"Havin' a good time?" Mamie asked when Sam joined her.

"Terrific. Thanks for including me."

Mamie looked her in the eyes. "Reckon I should be the one thankin' you."

"Gracious, what for?"

"For just bein' here. I ain't seen Ryder this relaxed in forever. You're good for 'im. May be pride talkin', but you could do a lot worse, honey."

"Oh, Mamie, I don't want you to think there's anything...permanent between us. I mean, we're just—"

"If you're gonna say good friends, save your breath. No man looks at a friend like Ryder looks at you. And you ain't 'xactly lookin' at him like a brother, either. Am I right or am I right?"

For the first time since she'd struck her deal with Ryder, Sam blushed. A part of her wanted to clarify the situation, but another part didn't want to risk Mamie's disapproval. "You're right."

Mamie grinned.

Not wanting the conversation to get any deeper, Sam pointed to the cake. "Need some help with that?"

"Sure. Them kids is probably 'bout to have a fit for a piece a cake." She cut two pieces, handed them to Sam.

Ryder was having a hell of a time concentrating. As much as he loved the game, poker couldn't hold a candle to watching Sam. The way she talked, walked. Especially the way she walked. Watching her move was like watching the breeze stir a willow tree on a summer evening. Slow, sensual. In fact, everything about her was sensual. Her smile, her voice. Oh, man, her voice, especially when she whispered, moaned. She smiled at him as she carried cake to the two kids, and he couldn't resist turning his head for an enticing view of her fanny in those great-fitting jeans. Suddenly, his own jeans were a little too snug for comfort. All he had to do was look at her and he was hard, and all he could think about was getting her back into bed.

"There you go." Sam handed each of the kids a plate, then turned to introduce herself to their mother. "I'm Sam Collins."

"Sam?"

"Short for Samantha."

"Oh. I'm Rosemary Booker." The woman shook her hand. "That tall one over there's Tom, my other half." She pointed to a man shooting pool with the young hand who had given up his seat at the table for Ryder.

"So nice to meet you. You've got beautiful kids," Sam told her.

"Oh, thank you, but you're seein' them on their best behavior tonight. Normally, they're a handful."

"How old are they?"

"Evie's six, and Tom Junior's eight."

Mamie joined them, and a sultry Faith Hill tune drifted from the jukebox. The pool game at an end,

Tom Booker walked over, grabbed his wife's hand and pulled her to a spot where they could dance. The young cowboy, Scooter, sat down with Sam and Mamie.

One moment Ryder glanced over his shoulder, saw Sam talking to Rosemary Booker, then it was his turn to call or raise. When he looked back a few moments later she was in Scooter Tompkins's arms, dancing. And Scooter was holding her like he was enjoying every minute. What the hell was going on? And if they just had to dance why weren't they doing the Cotton-Eyed Joe or a line dance instead of a slow two-step? And what the hell did Scooter think he was doing with his hand on Sam's hip?

"Hey," one of the players said. "You gonna play those cards, or strangle 'em?"

Ryder glanced down and discovered he had a death grip on his cards. "What? Oh, I'm in." He tossed some quarters into the center of the table without even counting them.

"Too rich for my blood," the next player announced.

Ryder looked back. They were still dancing, and Scooter was still holding her way too close. Then, to his relief, the music ended and Sam joined Mamie and the kids. That was more like it, he decided, and tried to get his mind on the game. It wasn't like him to fixate on a woman. He put it down to the fact that he'd been celibate for too long and that last night had been one of the most incredible nights he'd ever enjoyed with a woman. Naturally, he'd have sex on the brain.

And, just as naturally, he didn't like the idea of another man moving in on a woman he fancied.

They finished that hand and had just dealt another when Mamie ambled up, put her hand on Cotton's shoulder.

"You winnin' or what?" she asked him.

He smiled at her. "Breakin' even, sweet cheeks. And ain't you glad."

Ryder glanced over his shoulder, immediately whipped his head back around. "Where's Sam?"

"Oh, Scooter took her and the kids out to the barn to see the new puppies."

"Alone?"

"Told you. Scooter took 'em."

The play came around to Ryder. "I fold," he said and got up from the table.

Ryder noticed with chagrin that Mamie and Cotton exchanged glances and grins as he casually strolled out the French doors then took a hard left turn in the direction of the barn.

As he walked, Ryder told himself it was harmless enough. It wasn't like Scooter was taking her to the barn to make out. The Booker kids were with them, for crying out loud. Besides, it was none of his business. She was a grown woman. She could do whatever she wanted. All they had was a business deal. Nothing more. She was free to talk to whomever she chose. Scooter was a nice enough guy. A little cocky, maybe, but she couldn't have any real interest in him. He was just a kid.

Yeah. With a man's body and enough guts to use it. Ryder quickened his step.

IN THE BARN, Evie Booker climbed the outside of the stall and leaned over. "Oh, lookee," she squealed, seeing the nine bundles of fur cuddled next to their mother, a big, soft-eyed dog that looked like the result of an amorous misadventure between a golden retriever and a poodle.

Sam grabbed the back pocket of the child's jeans. "Careful. You might fall."

"You guys wanna hold one?" Scooter asked. To a chorus of "Can we, can we, can we?" he opened the stall, talking softly to the mother dog. "Hey there, Molly, girl. We just wanna check out a coupla your babies." Gently, he scooped up the two largest pups, placed one in Evie's arms and handed the other to Tom Junior. Then he reached down, collected the runt of the litter and gave it to Sam.

"Oh, my," she breathed. "I've never seen a puppy this young, much less held one." She stroked the tiny head and to her delight the puppy yawned and licked her finger. Sam laughed and held it up to her cheek to nuzzle. "You're so soft, so sweet."

"Just opened their eyes yesterday," Scooter said.

Evie and Tom Junior were busy with their charges and protested when Scooter told them they needed to return them to their mother. "She's gettin' restless for her young 'uns," he told them, taking each puppy. "You, too, runt." He reached for the pup Sam was holding, but as he pulled, the dog's sharp little nails snagged her hair.

"Oh, wait." Sam tried to disentangle herself and only made it worse. In her efforts she backed up against the stall door.

"Hold on," Scooter said and reached to help.

When Ryder walked into the barn all he saw was Sam smiling and Scooter facing her with his hands in her hair. "What the hell's going on here?"

At the sound of his voice the kids jumped down as if they thought they might be in trouble. "We were jest seein' the puppies," Evie explained.

"Scooter said it was okay." Tom Junior chimed in.

"Well, sure." Ryder kept his voice calm, level. No sense in making the kids feel as though they'd done anything wrong. "Y'all better run on back to the dining room now. Scooter'll take you."

"Sure, boss," Scooter said over his shoulder, his hands still in Sam's hair. "Just one sec. There you go," he told Sam. "You're a free woman."

"Thanks." She laughed, watching Scooter replace the pup.

Ryder knew he was being unreasonable, that it didn't make any sense, but that didn't change the fact that it took every ounce of his willpower not to pick the young cowboy up, toss him across the barn, then beat him to a pulp. To prevent that from happening, he only nodded as Scooter strolled by, collected the kids and walked out of the barn.

Still smiling, Sam looked at him. "The puppies are so cute, I—"

"You're not free."

"Pardon?"

"Not as long as you're on this ranch, in my bed."

For the first time she saw the expression on his face, fierce, black. "What are you talking about?"

"You and Scooter."

"Me and—"

"He had his hands on you."

"His hands? The puppy's little nails got tangled—" Suddenly, she realized all that blackness and fierceness were directed at her. "You thought we were...that something was going on?"

"Wasn't there?"

"No." For a heartbeat she was flattered, but the look in his eyes wasn't about flattery. It was all about anger.

He came toward her, stopped just shy of arm's length away. "I know what I saw."

"The puppy—"

"I don't give a damn about the dog!" Seeing her with Scooter, even thinking about another man touching her, had sparked something deep inside him. Something dark and frightening he couldn't understand, couldn't control. In a fury, he aimed it all at her.

"This is silly. He wasn't doing anything but helping untangle the puppy's claws from my hair."

Silly? It was another piece of timber on an already raging fire. He took a step forward, she took one back. The stall door was only inches from her back.

"Your deal is with me, not my hands. If one man isn't enough—" Her gasp cut him off and should have shut him up, but it was too late. "This is my ranch. We play by my rules."

She had enough sense to realize he was in a rage, but having never been in this position before, she didn't know how to react. So she did what she'd been conditioned to do—stand her ground. She straightened her shoulders, glared at him. "Your ranch. Your rules. Well, you—" she jabbed her finger in his chest "—are acting like an ass again. Deal or no deal, you don't have the right—"

She yelped in surprise when he grabbed her, hauled her backward, trapping her between the door and his body.

"You were more than willin' to give me the right last night. All the rights. Everything. Weren't you?" He all but shook her. "Weren't you?"

Suddenly everything was clear. He was angry with another woman, not her. He was a victim of his past. She should have been afraid, but something in his voice, almost desperation, touched her and made her fearless.

"Ryder. You don't have to worry. I'm not her."

His expression changed in a heartbeat, and he blinked. "Sam."

"Yes."

"Sam," he breathed, and pulled her into his arms. He held her close, tried to gentle the embrace but couldn't.

But she sensed that he didn't need gentle. He needed her. Just that quick the heat went through her, igniting, challenging her to meet the need, flame for flame. "Yes." She kissed his mouth, nibbled on his bottom lip.

Even as his mouth crushed hers he knew he should temper his need. But the fire burning out of control in his brain, his body, wouldn't let him. And she was at the heart of the fire. Proving he could control the blaze, making her part of it, got all mixed up with other feelings he couldn't identify. All he knew was that she was his. His alone. He wanted to put his brand on her so any man who looked at her would know she was his. Most of all, he wanted her to know it and want it.

His kiss was hot, demanding, nearly bruising. Whereas seconds ago she stiffened her body in defiance, now she was as pliable as warm wax, molding herself to him, clinging. Her fingers plowed through his hair, fisted there and held him fast. When he yanked her T-shirt out of her jeans, jerked it up and cupped her breasts, raw, naked desire roared through her like wildfire.

Without bothering to unhook her bra he freed her breast for the attention of his hot mouth, nipping, sucking at her flesh. He was possessed. Had to have her. Here, now. Only when he finally lifted his head to tell her so did he realize how close to madness he'd come. She looked at him, her mouth puffy from his ravaging kisses, her breathing short. The T-shirt was bunched over her collarbone, her bare breasts still damp from where he'd done everything but nip her with his teeth.

"I want..." Dazed and shocked at his behavior, he didn't know what to say to her.

No matter what he asked of her at that moment, she

only had one answer. "Yes. Oh, yes." She reached for him.

He caught both her hands. "Sam, I..." He shook his head as if he could shake off the fog of desire that had overtaken him. "Wait."

She looked at him, confused.

The confusion he saw in her eyes was nothing compared to the chaos in his brain at the moment. He'd never attempted to take a woman as he had a second ago. He'd been insensitive to the point of brutality. Never in his life had he treated a woman the way he'd just treated Sam. And to add to his confusion, she'd almost let him. He said the first thing that felt remotely logical. "We can't. Not in the barn."

"But—"

He tried to smile, but it came across almost as a grimace. "They'll probably send someone to look for us any minute."

"Oh." She was still breathing hard.

"I'm...sorry. I, uh, let things kinda get outta hand."

"It's...it's all right. I understand." But she didn't understand how he could turn off his desire so quickly. Her body still ached with need. Why didn't his?

He raised his hands in an effort to repair some of the damage he'd caused and discovered they were shaking. "You'd, uh, better fix your..." He gestured to her breasts.

"Oh, sorry." She turned away, not sure what she was apologizing for except that maybe she'd been too eager. By the time she'd fixed her bra and adjusted her shirt, he'd backed away. He didn't look at her.

"We'd better get back," he said, crammed his hands into his pockets and started to walk out of the barn.

Sam hurried after him. In fact, she had to race to keep up with his long stride. And for the rest of the evening she could feel his gaze on her, but whenever she glanced at him he looked away. For the life of her, she couldn't figure out what had gone wrong, but something surely had. Whatever the problem, it was important enough to Sam that she promised herself to resolve it before they went to sleep.

When the evening finally drew to a close, they said their good-nights and walked to the house. She was about to ask him what had happened when he kissed her. Softly, sweetly. The raging passion he'd shown in the barn was gone as if it had never existed.

"Why don't you go on in to bed. Got a couple of items that have to be taken care of before the computer company group arrives tomorrow. No reason for you to lose sleep."

"I thought they weren't due until right after noon."

"Yeah, but I've got a million things to do between now and then."

"Maybe I can help."

He shook his head. "Naw. It's just odds and ends."

"You're sure?"

"Positive."

She hesitated, waffling on her intention to talk about what had happened in the barn. Maybe this wasn't the time. He did have a lot on his mind, after all. And it was important to make every client happy if he was going to make the ranch successful. He had enough

stress without her adding to it. Tomorrow, she decided. Tomorrow would be soon enough.

"All right," she said and turned to leave.

"Sam."

She turned back. "Yes?"

"Sweet dreams."

She smiled and walked down the hall. When she got
to the guest room, again she hesitated. Where should
she sleep tonight? His room, or hers? After a moment,
she went into her room and closed the door.

Ryder heard the door close and knew she'd gone to
her own bed, not his. Maybe it was just as well, at least
for tonight. He'd never thought of himself as a jealous
man, but he'd sure as hell acted like one.

Women were for fun, good times and great sex. And
while that attitude might win him the label Champion
Chauvinist Pig, he was not, and never had been, abu-
sive. He'd never treated a woman badly in his life and,
until tonight, would have called any man who said he
might a liar. But something had snapped inside him
when he walked into that barn and saw Sam with
Scooter. Something that tapped a primitive need to
stake a claim, a fear of losing something he valued, and
he'd gone a little mad. He'd taken one look at her
and...

Old memories washed over him. He'd taken one
look at Sam and seen someone else.

He hadn't realized it, but Sam had. *I'm not her*. He'd
been so consumed with jealousy he hadn't remembered her words until now. Realizing he'd gotten
caught up in painful memories didn't account for why

he'd reacted so strongly. It wasn't as if he and Sam had been together for a long time. Or even came together out of mutual attraction. It was just sex. Great sex, but just sex.

Then why did he feel the need to go to her now, get down on his knees and beg her to forgive him? And why was her forgiveness suddenly so important? This was all happening so fast, and he wasn't sure exactly what *this* was. What he did know for certain was that, deal or no deal, he owed her an apology for being so rough with her tonight. After that, he had to find a way to get things back to where they were before he'd messed them up.

SAM WOKE UP ALONE, and long before the alarm went off. *All right*, she decided. The ball was in her court and she had no choice but to play it. Today, this morning, she had to talk to Ryder and find out what had happened last night. No matter what the answer, she had to know. Even if it meant the end of their deal? As much as she would wish otherwise, how could she go on with the arrangement the way things were? And she did want to go on with the arrangement. More than she'd realized until she faced the possibility that it might end. Sam hauled herself out of bed, showered, dressed and went to the kitchen. It was empty.

She found him in the barn, grooming one of the Shetland ponies provided for small children to ride. For a moment, she stood in the doorway, watching him. God, but he was magnificent. She loved the way he was built, all hard muscle and power. Loved the way he moved. And his hands... He had such wonderful, strong hands. She watched him brush the pony's coat, the muscles in his arms flexing. He stroked over and over until the little horse fairly gleamed and gave a shiver of pleasure. She knew what it was like to feel pleasure from those hands, to shiver in delight. No, she definitely wasn't ready to give Ryder up. She hoped she didn't have to.

"Good morning," she said, walking to the stall.

He looked up. "Mornin'."

"Who's your friend?"

"This is Prince." He stopped brushing, gave a gentle tug on the halter lead. "Say hello to the lady, Prince." The pony bobbed his head.

"Cute," Sam said. "Bet the kids love that."

"Yeah." He didn't resume the grooming, just stood there looking as if he didn't know what to say next.

"Ryder—"

"Sam, before you say anything I want you to know I've spent half the night and most of the morning trying to figure out the best way to apologize. When you get right down to it, there are only two words. I'm sorry."

"It's...it's all right."

"No, it's not. You were right. I acted like a prize jackass. If I'd seen anyone else treat a woman the way I treated you, I'd take him out behind the barn and beat him senseless. Good thing Cotton didn't see it, or he'd have done it to me." He took a step toward her. "I let some old pain make me stupid."

"I know."

"Yeah. You saw it right off, and I wanna thank you for understanding."

"You're only human, Ryder."

"Maybe, but there's no excuse for bein' rough with a woman, and it won't happen again. You got my word on that."

Relieved to have everything on an even keel, she put her hands in her pockets, rocked back and forth on her heels. "That's too bad," she said, slanting him a look from beneath her lashes.

"What?"

"I said, that's too bad. You seem to have forgotten I didn't exactly throw up my hands and run screaming into the night."

"You couldn't. I manhandled you. Women don't like that."

"It depends on the man." She stepped closer. "I'll admit I was—" she didn't want to use the wrong word, didn't want him to feel any worse "—surprised. But I'm a big girl, Ryder. You don't need to make decisions for me."

"Did I..." He reached a gloved hand to stroke her arm. "Did I hurt you?"

"No. And I never thought you would. Lighten up, Ryder."

The relief in his eyes almost made her want to cry. She could see the intensity lighten. "You see what I'm saying? Yes, you were angry. Yes, I was startled. *And* excited. If that makes me brazen, then you'll just have to live with it."

It was his turn to be surprised. He didn't know they

made women like her, but he was damn glad he'd been lucky enough to stumble across one. He looked at her for a long moment, the expression on his face moving from relief to questioning to acceptance. Finally, he smiled, his eyes sparkling. "Well, it's a tough job, but I guess somebody's gotta do it."

She sighed, relieved. "Thanks. And Ryder?"

"Yeah?"

"You're more than enough."

He looked at the barn floor, shook his head, then looked at her with a sexy grin. "You're full of surprises, you know that?"

"Just wanted you to know where I stood."

He nodded. "Sugar, after this, I'll never question it again."

Satisfied everything was back to where they both wanted it, Sam helped him finish grooming Prince, plus two more ponies.

"Is everything ready for the guests this afternoon?" she asked when they were done.

"For the most part. Depends on how many people decide they wanna ride. We're short a wrangler, but we can make do." They were about to walk out of the barn, when he stopped. "Can you ride?"

"Me? Horseback riding? Oh, Ryder, I'd love to help, but it's been a long time since I sat a horse. Better count me out. I'd hate to embarrass you in front of the guests."

"I'll let you off the hook today, but you can't really learn the ins and outs of a ranch on foot. First thing to-morrow, a refresher course."

"You got another deal." She offered a handshake.

He took her hand, but instead of shaking it, he pulled her into a darkened corner and kissed her.

It wasn't the kind of turbulent, arousing kiss they'd shared the night before, but in its own way it was just as disturbing. Sweet, soft and deep, it was a kiss of change, asking for and making promises neither would truly acknowledge.

Long after dark, when all the guests had finally gone and cleanup chores had been attended to, Ryder and Sam dragged their weary bodies to the house.

Sam collapsed in the first chair she saw. "How can something that looks like so much fun make every muscle in your body ache? And how do you survive working more than one of these things a week?"

Ryder laughed. "You get used to it."

"I'm a wimp. Even Cotton outworked me."

"Hey, don't be so hard on yourself." He walked behind her and began massaging her shoulders.

"Oh, dear Lord, that feels like heaven. Can you just stand there and do that for the next two or three hours?"

Ryder leaned down, kissed her neck. "I've got a better idea. How about we go to my room, take a nice hot shower, then you can stretch out on the bed for a full body massage?"

Slowly, she turned, looked at him. "Together?"

He cocked his head questioningly.

"Together in the shower?" she clarified.

He took her hand and pulled her into his arms. "Sounds like a hell of a plan to me."

"So, let me make sure I understand this plan. First a shower—"

"You wash my back, I wash yours…for starters."

"Hm. Then you give me a massage."

"Head to toe. Front to back."

"Then what?" she teased.

"Then—" he kissed her lightly, nibbling at her mouth until she sighed "—I'm thinking we might go ahead with that refresher course and see just how well you ride."

5

MONDAY MORNING Sam drove into Dallas to what used to be her office. She went straight to personnel, picked up her last paycheck, then asked one of the janitors if he had any boxes for her to pack her things, plus a dolly to haul them to her car. She had just taken her notes on the Copper Canyon appraisal out of her briefcase when Wendall Anderson walked past.

He stopped, obviously surprised to see her. "Oh, uh, Miss Collins. I, uh... You were out of the office Friday afternoon, weren't you?"

"Yes, sir." She could have let him off the hook and told him she knew about the layoffs, but she decided to get a little of her own back. Besides, he was so nervous he was sweating. Sam loved it. "You wanted that appraisal done in a hurry and—"

"Uh, yes. I remember now. Well, the fact is...I had assumed that someone would have told you by now."

"Told me what?"

"The, uh, company... Of course, you knew about the merger."

"Yes, sir."

"Well, unfortunately, it became necessary to, uh, let some employees go."

He stared at her, obviously hoping she would get the

message and save him the trouble of saying the words. Suddenly, a small taste of revenge wasn't enough for Sam. She wanted a full measure. Anyone who had a hand in disrupting people's lives should have to deal with at least one of those people face-to-face. He wasn't going to get away with a memo. "That's terrible. Did it involve a lot of people?"

"Quite...quite a few."

"Was Connie one of them?"

"Yes, I believe she was."

"I thought it was strange that she wasn't at her desk. She's rarely late." Sam shook her head, sincere regret in her eyes. "I don't know how I'll get along without her. She was my right arm."

"Miss Collins..."

"Yes?" It was all she could do to keep from grinning when he took out a handkerchief and wiped his hands. Sweaty palms were a thing of beauty, she thought. A joy to behold.

"I'm sorry, but you were terminated, as well."

Sam put her hand to her throat, deliberately made it tremble. "Oh," she whispered, her eyes wide. "I see."

"I thought you would hear through the grapevine. I certainly never expected you to show up this morning." He took a deep breath, put away his handkerchief. "But since you are here, it would be helpful if you could take a few minutes to finish the appraisal."

Of all the colossal gall, Sam thought. The man was too stupid to live and therefore not worth her time or vengeance. Well, maybe a little. "Under the circumstances that's going to take more time than I'm willing to give,

Mr. Anderson. But I will take my handwritten, and I'm afraid not very legible, notes and type them up." Like hell she would, Sam thought, and began collecting items from the top of her desk. "Oh, by the way—" she glanced at him. "—you might be interested to know that Mr. Wells already has someone interested in purchasing his property, and, I'm almost positive he told me, at a very nice price." She stepped around him. "Excuse me, I need to get some boxes from maintenance."

She should probably feel guilty for lying about Ryder having a buyer, but she didn't. Let Anderson stew over it for a while. As for her notes, he could wait until hell froze over as far as she was concerned, because they were going out of the office the same way they came in, tucked into her briefcase. It would be days, maybe even a week before he would think about looking for them. And it would take several more days of searching before he gave up and decided to reassign the appraisal. Take into consideration the backlog she knew existed, toss in human error, and Sam was betting Ryder would have enough time to save the ranch before the bank could take it. That made her smile. She'd also had the satisfaction of screwing up Anderson's day. That alone made it a good day's work.

An hour later she'd cleaned out her desk, seen the last of Frontier Financial Bank and was relieved to be on her way to Copper Canyon. It was strange that relief and freedom continued to be her strongest feelings about losing her job. Had she been so absorbed, so totally consumed by it that she hadn't realized how it had weighed her down, confined her? Obviously, the answer was yes, or she wouldn't feel the way she did. After only a few days without the constant pressure and struggle she felt better mentally and physically than she had in years. The drive for success that had been her companion since before she left the orphanage seemed to have shifted into neutral. A month ago she would have been frantic. Even a week ago she would have been so anxious about work, she wouldn't have been able to think of anything else. Now all she wanted was to be with Ryder at Copper Canyon Ranch.

SAM SPENT Monday afternoon working. She had Ryder's office to herself, since he was delivering a quarter horse he'd sold to a nearby rancher. By the close of the business day she'd received three bids, faxed or e-mailed, from prospective new vendors. If he decided to go with the new bids, the monthly savings would total over two hundred dollars. Not a lot in the grand scheme of things, but every little bit helped, and that was just the beginning. She hadn't even started looking for a new meat supplier, one of the three biggest expenditures. Next she intended to tackle feed bills, advertising, then personnel. Admittedly, she wasn't looking forward to that aspect of cost control. She knew it had to be done, but it wasn't going to be easy. Rosemary Booker and her two children came to mind. Socializing with Ryder's employees probably hadn't been a good idea, but now that she had, she couldn't imagine keeping herself aloof. The truth was, she didn't want to. A small voice inside her head reminded her not to lose her objectivity, but she was afraid it was already too late for that.

Close to sundown Sam left the office, pleased with the day's work. She didn't see Mamie or Ryder anywhere, so she strolled toward the corral. The high school boys were back, practicing falling from their horses as if they'd been shot. Sam smiled. The grown-up version of cowboys and Indians.

Cotton was at his familiar stand, watching. "Hi," she said as she walked up.

"Hey there, Sam. Ain't seen you all day."

"I've been busy saving Ryder some money."

He grinned. "I knew you was gonna be good fer him. So, you think we can hang on to this place?"

"It's not quite that easy. I've barely put a dent in what needs to be done and, frankly, my biggest worry is time. I'm just not sure we have enough."

"You jest do the best you can. That's all a body can ask."

"We really need an investor, but—"

"Yeah. I'll bet Ryder put the kibosh on that mighty quick."

"Yes, he did."

"He don't want nothin' to do with partners. Even turned me down."

"You?"

"Me and Mamie come to him not six months ago. Told him he could have whatever we got. You shoulda seen the fit he pitched. Stampin' and snortin' like a rank bull. Said he'd be six feet under 'fore he'd take our old-age money. Hell," Cotton said, "don't he know he's like our own?"

"I think he does know, Cotton, but it's hard for him to let go of any part of this place to anybody, even people he loves."

"Yeah, I reckon. Hardheaded jackass."

"Would you have him any other way?" Sam asked.

Cotton shook his head. "Wouldn't if I could. Besides, he come by it natural like. His daddy and granddaddy was cut from the same piece of tough boot leather."

"Why am I not surprised," she said, and they both laughed.

One of the riders executed a fancy dismount less than two yards from where they stood. The young man doffed his hat and bowed to Sam. When she smiled and applauded, he hopped on the horse and took off at a gallop toward his friends.

"He's very good," she told Cotton.

"Damn good. The best, in fact. All them boys bug Ryder for tips, but that one, name's Ellis, takes it real serious. Been comin' out here regular for over a year. Says he wants to go be a stuntman."

"You think he'll do it?"

Cotton shrugged. "Ryder says he's got the talent and the brains. And God knows he's worked hard enough. Graduatin' high school the end o' this month with honors. Says he's gonna take hisself off to a stunt school soon as he gets enough money saved up."

"I didn't know such places existed."

"Reckon so."

"Did Ryder go to one of those schools?"

"Nope. Learned the hard way. Hooked up with some fella in the business that taught him."

"You know, he's never talked too much about what he used to do before taking over the ranch."

"I reckon he's got enough on his plate thinkin' 'bout the future to spend much time thinkin' 'bout the past.

"Speaking of Ryder, where is he?"

He motioned toward the house. "Last time I saw him, Mamie had 'im pinned up in the laundry room givin' him what for on account he didn't fix the washer like he said he was gonna." Cotton looked toward the house. "Guess his mind's been on other things," he said and chuckled.

RYDER KNEW COTTON had seen him and could predict what was going through his old friend's mind. Some thoughts along the line of why didn't he snap up this fantastic woman before someone else did. In only three short days both Cotton and Mamie had taken Sam in as if she was a member of the family. That bothered him. He and Sam weren't lovers. Well, not in the traditional sense. And he didn't want things to get...cozy. He wasn't interested in cozy unless it involved cozying up to Sam in bed. That was the deal, and that's how he wanted it to stay.

He shook his head. He'd never met a woman like her. She was honest, plainspoken, smart as a whip and without a coy bone in her body. Definitely not the kind of woman he usually spent time with. And she sure as hell was a world away from Alicia. Trust issues. Isn't that what Sam had said? Yeah, he had trust issues, and he'd hung on to them for over a year. And they had protected him from making another mistake. When it came to women, he kept his mind clear, his money close and his heart hidden. Maybe that's why he was still trying to figure out why he was allowing Sam access to his books, his business. The truth was, aside from the sex thing, he felt at ease with her and had from the first. The mere fact of her presence had ticked him off in the beginning, but he'd have felt the same resentment toward any appraiser, male or female. No, there was something about Sam that inspired trust, whether a person wanted to be inspired or not. And while that thought made him ponder, it didn't cause the anxiety he expected.

"She's okay fer a city gal," Mamie said, walking up to stand beside him.

"Think so?"

"I do. Don't hurt none that she's pretty, too. And smart, I reckon."

"A hell of a lot smarter than me, it seems."

Mamie grinned at him. "Well, that ain't hard to do."

"Gee, thanks."

"I meant where ladies are concerned. You can charm 'em right outta their frilly underwear, but you're a lousy picker."

"Picker?"

"Yeah, you can't pick yourself a woman." She grabbed the coffeepot and poured them both a fresh cup. "Leastways not a good one."

"You're an expert on my women now?"

She thought for a moment. "Nope. You jest naturally

latch on to ones that lie to get what they want. But you better watch yore step with that one out there." She pointed to Sam. "She's the real deal."

The real deal, he thought as Mamie walked away. She was real sexy, for sure. And, for now, that's as real as he wanted to get.

He had just about finished his job for Mamie. A few minutes later, he joined Cotton outside.

"Well, now," Cotton said. "Here comes the boss. 'Bout time you showed up to help me unload that trailer." He pointed to a trailer piled high with bales of hay, hitched to Ryder's pickup.

"What's this? My two top hands loafin'?" Ryder teased.

"Oh, yeah. Jest been sittin' in a rockin' chair all day. Ain't that right, Sam?"

"Absolutely."

"Well, since you're so rested, guess you'll be taking Mamie to the VFW hall to play bingo then."

Cotton groaned. "I plumb forgot this was the night. Hey, y'all wanna go with us?"

"Uh, well…" Sam glanced away, not particularly interested but unsure how to get out of going without hurting Cotton's or Mamie's feelings.

"We'll take a rain check," Ryder said. "I promised Sam I'd teach her how to play poker."

Sam's head came up. "That's right, you did. And you never make a promise you can't keep, right?"

Ryder's gaze bored into her, hot as a July day. "Right. Want to ride up to the barn with me while I unload the trailer?"

"Sure." With a wave to Cotton, she climbed into the truck. "That was close," she told Ryder.

"Good thing for you I think fast."

"Speaking of fast, there's a good chance I saved you some money today."

"Atta girl."

"I've just scratched the surface, though. We've still got a long way to go. What are you doing?" she asked when, instead of stopping at the barn, he pulled around behind it and killed the truck's engine.

"Something I've been thinking about doing all day."

"And what's that?"

He crooked a finger at her. "C'mere."

Sam scooted across the seat. "All right, now what's—"

He hauled her across his lap and kissed her before she could finish whatever she intended to say. And he kept on kissing her until she couldn't breathe, couldn't think. When he reached for the buttons on her shirt she protested only slightly.

"Somebody might see us."

"Why do you think I parked back here? I've got—" he opened her shirt "—to have just—" pushed it aside "—one taste." He ran his tongue over the soft swell of her breasts, tasted, teased to his heart's content before returning to her mouth.

Desire sprang inside her, quick, hot. She'd never known anything like the instantaneous need that hit her every time he touched her. But then, she'd never known a man like Ryder. He made her feel soft, sexy and powerful all at the same time. Heady stuff, and she couldn't get enough.

He lowered his head, planted kisses on her throat, earlobes. "Ever made love in the back seat of a car?" he asked, his voice husky.

"This is a truck, and—" Her breath caught when he pushed her bra down and took her nipple in his mouth. "Ryder." She reached to pull him closer, but the sound of voices stopped her.

The boys who had been working with their horses earlier in the corral were walking behind the truck. "Damn," Ryder muttered. He yanked Sam's shirt together even as she slithered out of his lap, trying to right herself. "No way they won't stop to talk if they see us."

Shoving buttons through buttonholes as fast as she could, Sam scrambled to the passenger side of the truck. She pushed her hair away from her face and tried to look normal. They both sat still, expecting recognition, but the boys were so busy talking to each other they walked past without even noticing Sam and Ryder.

Sam didn't realize she'd been holding her breath until they'd gone. When Ryder reached for her again, she put up a hand. "Oh, no. I'll risk a lot of things, but being the hottest piece of gossip in a boy's high school locker room isn't one of them."

Ryder laughed. "Killjoy."

"I think we better unhitch the trailer and go to the house."

"Well, you're gonna have to give me a minute,

sugar. Right now, I can't walk three steps." For the first time since he'd met her, she blushed. "So, to get my mind off you, why don't you tell me how you saved me money today."

She told him about the bids and about her plans to check out a new meat supplier and take a hard look at the advertising. While she talked, Ryder listened, and with each passing minute he realized he'd underestimated her commitment to helping him. She had a step-by-step plan complete with timetable and alternatives. After the rundown, he was ready to unhitch the trailer.

"I need to go online after supper to check out some information on grants," Sam told him as they walked to the house.

"Grants?"

"Of course. There's a lot of money available if you know where to look and how to qualify. The third, no, fourth job I ever had was working for the college I attended handling requests for grants and student loans."

"What did you do before that?"

"Let's see. My first job was the summer I turned fifteen, as a maid baby-sitter housekeeper—notice I didn't say cook—for a family with two kids. The second was at a bakery, at the cash register, all through high school. The third, and shortest lived, was modeling for the art department my first year in college."

"Modeling?"

"Life modeling. It all sounded just fine until the professor told me I would have to be nude."

Ryder grinned. "I knew you were a hot number."

"Needless to say, the sisters at the orphanage made sure that was the shortest employment in history."

"Do you mind if I ask what happened to your family? I mean, if you don't want to—"

"No, it's all right. I was told that my parents were killed in a car accident before I was a year old. An aunt, my mother's sister, took care of me for a couple of years, but she developed cancer. There was nobody else, so she made arrangements for me to go into a Catholic orphanage in San Antonio. I think my father must have been an only child, because there's no information about his family."

"That's rough."

She shrugged. "You can't miss something you've never had." That had been true until a few days ago. Suddenly an unexpected pang of loneliness sliced through her as she thought about the fact that she would eventually have to leave. She pushed the thought away. "What about you? Cotton told me your dad passed away last year." She'd deliberately not mentioned his mother, mainly because Cotton hadn't. Maybe Ryder's mother had left, or maybe it was a family secret no one discussed.

"I don't talk about my family much."

"Forgive me. I didn't mean to pry."

"No, it's all right. I guess I don't talk about them much because I try not to think about them much." Remembering had always been too painful, but somehow it seemed right to tell Sam. He didn't even stop to think why, he just knew it did.

Almost as if he was slowly easing into his memories,

he slowed his pace. "My mom died when I was four. Cancer, like your aunt."

On the verge of offering sympathy, Sam noticed he'd slowed his pace even more and glanced away, as if he was trying to decide whether or not to say more. She waited.

"I had an older brother," he said finally, his voice as rusty as a hinge on a seldom used door. "Twelve years older, in fact. My folks thought they couldn't have any more kids, then I came along. Cliff, that's my brother, was killed in a rodeo accident while I was still in grade school." There was another long stretch of silence before he spoke again.

"He was a bull rider. Real good at it, too. He was competing in a small rodeo in Tyler. Outdoor arena. It'd come a real gully washer the night before. After the buzzer sounded, Cliff jumped off. The bull was still buckin' and jumpin' all over the place. Cliff tried to get out of the way, but the bull slipped, fell on him. He died a few hours later."

"You saw it." It wasn't a question. Listening to his choppy sentences, his controlled breathing, it was clear the memory was painful. Too painful not to have been firsthand.

"He was covered in mud. I...I couldn't see his face when they put him in the ambulance. They wouldn't let me see him later." Ryder took a deep, shuddering breath. "Sometimes when it rains..." But he didn't finish.

"Oh, Ryder, I'm so sorry. So very sorry."

"It's—"

Instinctively, she reached out and took his hand. "Don't say it's all right. It couldn't be. You were just a kid, and you probably looked up to your brother, even worshiped him. And to lose him like that had to be more than you could bear. It still must be."

He looked at her as if surprised that she understood, and she wondered if he'd ever told his family about his pain.

"Cotton drove me to the hospital that night," he said, as if that explained everything else. In a way, it did. Nothing had ever been the same after that, certainly not his relationship with his dad. Art Wells hadn't turned a cold shoulder, just retreated in a way Ryder had never been able to understand, much less change. Slowly but surely, Cotton West had become a surrogate for his distant father.

Ryder took another deep, cleansing breath. He hadn't talked about any of this for years, and as painful as the memories still were, it was good to get them out. Somehow, holding Sam's hand made it easier. "Cliff was helping Dad run the ranch while he was still in diapers, so the story goes. Afraid I was only a runner-up. Got the job by default, you might say. And never quite measured up."

"But you love this place."

"Yeah, I do. But it took me a lot of years to get there. Cliff left some big shoes to fill, and me, I hated the whole idea of *having* to be what my dad wanted me to be. So every time he talked about me takin' over, I dug my heels in that much more against it. Didn't figure I could ever be as good as my brother, so I decided the only way I could stand my own ground was to leave."

"And become a stuntman."

He nodded, grateful to move away from the painful memories. "Spent some of the best years of my life jumpin' off roofs, being shot at, set on fire and doing the most dangerous stunts they could dream up."

"And that was fun?"

"Oh, man, was it."

"It would scare me senseless."

"That's what makes it so much fun."

"Do you miss it?"

"Honestly, yeah. Sometimes I miss the action, the excitement. But I sure as hell don't miss L.A. or memories connected to it. Anyway, Texas is home." They stopped at the back door. "Took me a while to realize how important that is. How important this place is. And I'm gonna fight like hell to keep it."

"We've got a shot at it, Ryder. And I'm going to do everything I can to make it happen."

"Thanks." When she started to go in he tugged on her hand, stopping her. "You know, this deal of ours started out kinda fast and wacky, but I just wanted to tell you that no matter how it turns out, I'm glad you showed up, glad your car broke down and real glad you had a yen for a fling."

"Me, too."

Mamie was taking a meat loaf out of the oven when they walked into the kitchen. "'Bout time y'all showed up. Sam, the gravy's made, fresh green beans in the pot and the bread's bakin'. All you got to do is mash them taters—" she pointed to one of the pans on the stove "—and you can eat. Reckon you can handle that. I got to get myself cleaned up for bingo," she said with a broad smile. "Don't get that old coot I married to take me out but once in a blue moon. Gotta take while the takin's good."

"Have a great time," Sam told her.

"I aim to do jest that," Mamie said as she whipped off her apron and headed out the door.

"Are you hungry?" Sam asked when there were just the two of them.

"Actually, I am. Need any help?"

"You heard Mamie, all that's left is to mash the potatoes. While I do that, why don't you go into the office and take a look at those bids I mentioned?"

"Good idea."

Forty-five minutes later they had finished their meal and were lingering over coffee. "You know what?" Sam said, rubbing her neck. "On second thought, I'm going to skip the research until tomorrow morning. And after I clean up this kitchen, I think I'm going to run a bubble bath and soak for a while."

"Go on," Ryder told her. "I'll take care of this for you."

"Are you sure?"

"Hey, I can throw plastic wrap around food and wipe a countertop with the best of them. How do you think I survived on my own all those years?"

"Girlfriends?"

"Well—" he grinned "—won't deny I had help occasionally."

"You don't have to offer twice. Thanks."

"Just leave enough hot water for me," he called as she disappeared down the hall.

Liberally sprinkling the bath salts she'd purchased, Sam ran a tub of pleasantly hot water. Then she lit several candles, pinned her hair atop her head, peeled out of her clothes and stepped in. She sighed in pure pleasure as she slid into the silky suds up to her chin.

Pure pleasure, she thought, breathing in the scented steam. That described her whole day, even the part involving the bank. She felt as if some oppressive weight had been lifted from her shoulders. Her step was light, her mind clear. No regrets. Especially not where Ryder was concerned.

She thought about their conversation and how his life had been filled with as much grief as hers. She'd always considered people with families to be so fortunate, so blessed. Her heartache had always been not having one. She'd never really stopped to consider that it could be equally heartbreaking to have a family and disappoint them, or worse, not appreciate them until it was too late. Remembering the past, talking about it, couldn't have been easy for Ryder. The fact that he'd chosen to share that part of himself with her made her feel special. More than just part of a deal.

There she went again, fantasizing. She scooped a double handful of bubbles, brought them to her face and blew. Clusters of bubbles spurted into the air, popping, disappearing—a good representation of her chance at anything more with Ryder than their bargain. She needed to stick to that bargain and forget about silly, romantic fantasies that couldn't come true. A deal was a deal.

"You gonna stay in there all night?"

Sam jumped at the sound of Ryder's voice, almost sending water and bubbles over the edge of the tub. "You scared me. How long have you been standing there?"

"Couple of minutes. Just enjoying the view, sugar."

Actually, he'd hurried through his shower and had been watching her for several minutes. He'd intended to announce his presence, but when he saw her sitting there, bubbles up to her chin, the candlelight making her skin glow, he'd lost the power of speech. It was like seeing her that first night. The same punch-to-the-gut reaction had him staring at her, wanting her every bit as much as he had that first night. But different. Before tonight he probably wouldn't have thought twice about crossing to the tub, lifting her out, carrying her to his bed and making love to her, bubbles and all, until they were both senseless. But tonight that wasn't enough. Telling her about Cliff had changed something. He wasn't sure exactly what, but things were different. He was different. Maybe it was the compassion and understanding he'd seen in her eyes. The sympathy without pity. Or maybe...

He could recite maybes all day long, but the truth was, he knew exactly when the change had happened, and why. Her hand had touched his, and without him telling her, she'd known how much he'd been hurt. How much he still hurt. He hadn't felt that kind of soul-deep connection to anyone in a long time. It scared him, yet he was reluctant to turn his back on it. He only knew he wanted tonight to be more than just quick sex. He wanted to please her before he pleasured her.

"Well," she asked, when he didn't move away from the door. "Are you going to hand me my towel or just stand there and watch me drip-dry?"

"Tempting." He handed her the towel. "But I've got a better idea."

"Oh, really?"

"Slip into that sexy gown. Then a robe and slippers."

"But—"

"Then come into my room. I've got a surprise."

Her face lit up like a child's on Christmas morning. "A surprise? Tell me."

"Nope." He turned and walked out of the room.

"Ryder? Ryder Wells, you come back here!" When he didn't answer, she climbed out of the tub and hastily dried herself off. She had just thrown her night-gown over her head and was about to run after him when she stopped, changed her mind. It would be a shame to spoil the surprise. Grinning, she slipped into her robe, pulled the sash tight around her waist, stepped into her slippers and all but ran to Ryder's room. And came to a screeching halt in the doorway.

He was stretched out on the king-size bed, propped up on one elbow, fully dressed and shuffling a deck of cards.

"You said you wanted to learn how to play poker," he told her, casually cutting the cards.

"This is my surprise?"

He nodded.

"But I thought we were going to—"

"Yeah, I know what you thought we were going to do. Now, you wanna learn this game or not?"

"Absolutely," she said, warming to the scenario.

"Since I'm feeling generous tonight, I'm giving you exactly three minutes to find more clothes to put on. To stack the deck, you might say."

"Generous, indeed. When do my three minutes start?"

He looked at his watch. "Now."

Almost giggling, Sam rushed to her room, flung open a drawer and rummaged around until she found what she wanted. She ran back to the room just as he said, "Time."

"Done," she said, breathlessly.

"I don't see anything more than you had on when you left."

"Not yet, you don't."

Ryder's smile was nothing short of triumphant.

"And you won't unless you win."

"Oh, I intend to win, all right. Make no mistake."

She sat down on the bed. "Then deal."

"Not so fast, sugar. First, you learn the rules."

"I'm all yours." She leaned forward just enough so that her robe gaped open to reveal her gown and something else beneath it.

"I'll hold you to that."

"This is going to be fun. Are we going to play Texas Hold 'Em?"

She had that same twinkle in her eyes like a kid on

Christmas morning that he'd seen a moment ago. "That's the advanced course. We'll start with just plain old draw poker. To begin with, there's one joker in the deck, and aces can be played high or low for a straight. Know what a straight is?"

She thought for a moment. "Uh, ace through five of the same suit, or ten through ace."

"Right. Three of a kind, two pair, one pair, high card—all self-explanatory."

"And for betting, we use—"

"Clothes, shoes, whatever we've got on."

Sam smiled and rubbed her hands together. "Let's play."

6

"YOU GONNA RAISE or call?" Ryder asked.

"Don't rush me. What's the bet?"

"My right boot and my belt buckle."

"I still say separating the belt and the buckle isn't fair." Sam looked at her cards again.

"Did I say anything when you bet one earring, then another? Now, what are you gonna do?"

"I'll see your boot and raise you my other slipper."

"I call."

Sam smiled and laid down her cards. "Two pair," she said proudly.

"Sorry, sugar." He showed his hand. "Three of a kind. So far, you've lost both earrings, both shoes and your watch. Looks like the robe is next."

"*If* you win."

He chuckled. "If?"

They'd played three practice hands, two of which Sam had won. But things changed when they started playing for real. So far, Ryder had only lost one hand and forfeited one boot. Sam, on the other hand, was almost down to bare essentials. "Are you sure you're not cheating?"

"Sugar, you cut me to the quick. I'm telling you, it's just the luck of the draw. Of course, for a woman with your skill with numbers I would've thought you'd do better at this game."

"So did I." She shuffled the cards, dealt each of them two, one face up.

"I'll bet my shirt," Ryder said.

Sam looked at him for a moment and decided it was time to turn losing to her advantage. "Take it off," she said.

"What?"

"You heard me. Take it off. I've decided we should put our bets on the table. Uh, bed."

Without breaking eye contact, he sat up and slowly began unsnapping his shirt. First one snap, then two. "You sure you wanna do this?" More snaps popped. "That means you'll have to ante up, as well."

"I know."

The shirt undone, he slipped it off and dropped it onto the bed in a heap. Sam let out her breath slowly, admiring his broad chest and shoulders. Her fingers itched to touch him. "You're a hunk, did you know that?"

Ryder grinned. "I'll take your word for it." When she reached out to touch his bare shoulder, he leaned back and wagged his finger at her. "Not until you win the pot."

Her gaze narrowed. "Oh, you're going to pay for that. Big time."

"Promises, promises. It's one shirt to you."

"I'll see your shirt." She peeled out of her robe, neatly folded it, then put it beside his shirt. "And raise you." Then she stood up, reached for the hem of her gown and slowly began pulling it up her body.

Ryder held his breath as the silk nightgown slithered up her legs, revealing a pair of the skimpiest black bikini panties he'd ever seen, then up over her narrow waist and rib cage, uncovering a black lace bra. She folded the gown and set it atop the robe. She was absolutely, positively the most beautiful thing he'd ever seen. "Is that what you put on when I gave you the chance to stack the deck?"

Slowly, she turned in a circle. "You like?"

Ryder laughed. "Are you crazy? I love it."

"Thought you might."

"The only place that little bit of nothing you're wearing would look better than it does right now is stacked up on this pile." He pointed to the shirt and robe.

"We'll see." Sam stretched out on the bed facing him, propped herself on her elbows and dealt them each another card, face up. Then she leaned forward as if studying her hand. "Hmm," she said, giving him an unobstructed view of her breasts barely contained by black lace. "Let me think." She leaned back and lightly tapped one corner of a card against her bottom lip for a second, then looked to be sure he was drooling sufficiently. He was. "Why don't you raise with your jeans? If you've got a decent hand, that is."

He knew she was trying to drive him crazy, and she was very close to succeeding. Knowing all he had to do was reach out, push a bit of lace out of the way to have her fully exposed to his greedy gaze was testing his limit. "Sugar, if I take these jeans off the game's over."

"You think that'll distract me, make me forget I've got a winning hand?"

"I know it will."

She flipped a mass of curls away from her face, arching her back in the process. "So sure of yourself, aren't you?"

"Sure enough." But he wasn't sure which would pop out first—her breasts or his eyes.

Enjoying herself thoroughly, Sam knew it was just a matter of time before neither of them could stand not touching the other, but a little devil was riding on her shoulder. She couldn't resist pushing her advantage to the limit. "So—" she took a deep breath, her breasts straining against the lacy confinement, then exhaled slowly "—I suppose I'll have to raise the ante."

Ryder's gaze was like an intense blue flame as it traveled down the length of her body, then back up. "You've raised everything else."

"Hmm, yes. It does seem to have warmed up in here."

"And getting hotter by the minute." He'd gotten a real kick out of the teasing at first. Now he was eager for it to end. Eager to have her beneath him, begging for him. The only thing that stopped him from taking her this very minute was the fun she was having.

"Let's see." She ran her index finger along the edge of one bra strap, toying with it until it slipped off her shoulder. "What shall I bet?" Her hand moved to the bikini panties, skimmed the elastic edge. Then she slipped her finger beneath the elastic as if to push the panties down. "Maybe not," she said. "I think I should—"

"That's it." Cards flew everywhere even as he reached for her.

"Hey," she protested as they tumbled over on the bed, laughing. She put her hands on his shoulders as if to fend him off. "I was just about to win that hand."

"You were just about to drive me straight to the funny farm."

"Short trip. Give me my cards."

He rolled her beneath him, trapping her. "No."

And just that quick the laughter died, the teasing ceased.

"Now what are you gonna do?" he murmured, his voice low, smooth as velvet.

Sam looked into his heart-stopping blue eyes, and something in her moved, shifted, as if she'd stepped into another realm of reality. One that had less to do with the body and more to do with the heart. She wanted him, yes. But in that moment she realized she wanted all of him, the same way she wanted to give him all of her. Heart, mind, body and soul. She wanted to make love to him, be loved by him...

Because she loved him.

A simple declarative sentence. Four profound words that changed her world, turned it upside down...then cast a cloud over it. As wonderful as loving Ryder sounded, it could only be one-sided. He was only interested in their deal. Their short-term deal.

Ryder saw the expression in her eyes change to something he couldn't fathom. The desire was still there, but deeper. No, not even that. It was as if he was watching a rare, exquisite flower blossom right in front of his eyes into something so beautiful, so glorious it was almost beyond description. But tinged with a sadness at the same time. He was humbled by that beauty, curious about the sadness and totally in awe of this woman.

"Ryder," she whispered, aching with love for him, desperately needing to show what she dared not speak.

Maybe it was the look in her eyes or the way she said his name, but what had started out as just for fun was now startlingly serious. The feeling he'd experienced when she'd touched his hand, voiced his pain, came rushing back, only more intense. He'd only wanted to please her before he pleasured her. Now he wanted to make love to her. If he had stopped to think about that for a moment, he might have been scared witless. But he wasn't thinking, didn't want to. All he wanted was her. More than he'd ever wanted anything in his life. His body still covering hers, gently he kissed her soft mouth. There was no need to hurry, only to savor. And he did, slowly, tenderly, loving her well into the night.

SAM SAT STARING at the computer screen, as she had for the past hour, trying to get her mind around the fact that she was in love with Ryder. It was shocking, unsettling and astounding all at the same time. So unsettling that she'd had a hard time making small talk during breakfast. So astounding that all she wanted to do was revel in the feeling, savor the moment. But it was also disaster, and she knew it. Only fools fall in love so fast. Well, then she was a fool. Her only saving grace was that Ryder didn't know. Couldn't know. Besides, there was no reason he should. After all, it wasn't her heart that interested him. They had a business deal. The question was, how was she going to hold up her end of their deal knowing she was in love with him? More important, how was she going to make love with him without doing just that? What if he could tell just by the way she touched him, kissed him? What if he confronted her with the truth? Or, maybe worst of all, what if he didn't see anything but what he wanted to see?

What if, what if, what if…

She would make herself crazy trying to see into a future that could really only have one ending. In a few more days she would leave Ryder and Copper Canyon Ranch, and that would be that. Where was her new-found resolve to go for the adventure in life? To have fun? This whole thing was her idea, after all. If she slipped into an emotional quagmire, she had no one to blame but herself.

"Stay focused," she announced to the computer screen. "That's what I have to do." Stay focused on the job at hand. Find a way to help Ryder.

Cotton stuck his head in the door. "Hey, there."

"Hey," she said, relieved to have something else to deal with. "What's up?"

"Ryder sent me with a message. Promised the boys to show 'em some fancy falls 'n stuff. Wants to know if you wanna watch?"

"Oh, yes, I do. Now?"

"You betcha."

Grateful for the distraction, she smiled and followed him out of the house to his truck. A few moments later she and Cotton rolled to a stop at the arena used to entertain the guests with a small rodeo. An announcer's stand was situated at one end of the arena, and Ryder had already set up a huge air bag beneath it. He and two of the boys were standing alongside the air bag. Ryder looked up and waved at Sam as she got out of the truck. He was wearing his usual attire, jeans, boots and a T-shirt, but there was nothing usual about the way the man looked. Handsome as sin, she thought. Just your average mouthwatering hunk. She waved and tried not to think about how much she loved him.

"Now you're gonna see somethin'," Cotton said. "Ryder makes it look easy as fallin' off a log."

Sam gauged the height of the announcer's stand. "A log ten or fifteen feet off the ground. Isn't this dangerous?"

"Some, I reckon, but he's done it so long, he never gets hurt."

"What about the boys? What happens if they get hurt?"

"Ryder thought 'bout that right off. Talked to all the boys' folks, and they all signed one of them whatchamacallits." He scratched his head, dislodging his hat. "Aw, hell, a piece of paper sayin' they wouldn't hold Ryder responsible if anythin' happened. Besides, them boys done learned how to fall off a horse, so this oughtta be a piece a cake."

"I see." But she wasn't looking at Cotton, she was watching Ryder instruct one of the boys on how to fall. Once, twice, he jumped from the highest rail of the fence surrounding the arena, expertly landing on the air bag. The boy tried it, messed up the first two tries, but got it the third. Ryder set the boy to practicing while he instructed the second boy, Ellis. Ellis got it the first time, but continued to practice. For the next ten minutes the boys jumped, landed, then safely rolled off the air bag. Finally satisfied with their ability, Ryder led them up to the announcer's stand. He jumped from that height, again landing like the expert he was.

As Sam watched and applauded first one boy's efforts, then the next, she thought about how patient Ryder was with them. How he explained everything, emphasizing safety, tailoring his instructions so that each boy was able to fully understand. He was a great teacher. Granted, he knew these boys and had worked with them for a while, but he was good. Good enough to teach...

Anybody.

Anybody with enough money to pay for expert instruction.

Suddenly, she had an idea. So simple, so obvious, she couldn't imagine why no one had thought of it before. And, if it worked, the answer to saving the ranch was practically staring them in the face. Excited and eager to check out her idea but not wanting to mention it until she had more to go on, she couldn't wait to get back to the computer.

"Cotton, I hate to drag you away, but I just remembered something I have to take care of. Could you drive me back to the house?"

"Go on and take the truck. I'll come back with Ryder and the boys."

Feeling like hugging him, she settled for a wide grin instead. "Thanks, Cotton. Thanks."

Ten minutes later she was online, searching for every piece of information she could find about stunt schools, locations, operations and income possibilities. She kept at it the rest of the morning, ate at her desk and worked until Mamie showed up and insisted she take a break. After almost four hours of solid searching from Web site to Web site, she had to admit her eyes were tired and she'd acquired several knots across her neck and shoulders. But it was all worth it. Everything she'd found only made her more excited about the idea of turning Copper Canyon Ranch into Copper Canyon Stunt School. Still, there was a lot to be done before she could present her idea to Ryder. Money, for one thing. It would take a lot to do what needed to be done, but with Ryder's background and credentials, it was possible—a much stronger possibility than getting another loan for a floundering guest ranch.

Why hadn't she thought of this before? Why hadn't Ryder?

Then it hit her that maybe he had. Maybe he'd rejected the idea because he didn't want any part of that business anymore. At that, her excitement wilted. Running a stunt school made perfect sense to her, but it might not be what Ryder wanted at all. Well, there was only one way to find out. Tonight, after dinner, she would go to him with all the information she'd collected and her proposed plan in hand. If he didn't like the idea of a stunt school, that was that. But if he did, she would have hard facts and figures to show him.

Sam cautioned herself against getting too wrapped up in her idea, but it was hard not to be. She wanted to help Ryder so much, and this looked like such a logical, workable answer to his problem. In fact, she knew it might be the only solution. There wasn't enough time to turn the guest ranch around. Her biggest stumbling block was advertising. For the guest ranch to succeed, he had to commit to full-scale advertising. And that took money. Lots of money. There was always the chance of getting another loan, perhaps a small one to cover advertising, but it was iffy. And since he had vetoed an investor, she was working at a disadvantage. Ryder knew that. He hadn't gone into their deal blindly—desperately, maybe, but not without knowing the reality of the situation. So had Sam. But for her, reality took a hard left turn last night. Her perspective, her direction had changed. There was a world of difference between wanting to solve a problem, make something work for someone she liked and respected, and doing it for someone she loved. Wasn't the basis of real love wanting the best for the loved one, even if that didn't include you? If that made her a fool, then so be it.

Deciding she'd done all she could do for now, Sam collected the sheets of information she'd printed out and stuffed them into a manila envelope. If Ryder liked her idea, the only negative as far as she was concerned was that she wouldn't be around to see it through. That was more painful than she would have thought possible only a few short days ago. But a few days ago she hadn't been in love. Sam sighed, put the envelope on the corner of Ryder's desk, then followed her nose to the kitchen where the smell of cookies baking had beckoned for the last half hour.

"You sure know how to make a girl forget about work," Sam said as she walked into the fragrant room.

"'Bout time you stuck your nose outta that office." Mamie held up a plate heaped high with fresh-baked chocolate chip cookies. "Have some. They're good for what ails you."

"They're good, period." She helped herself to two.

"Laid out a couple a steaks for you and Ryder," Mamie said, storing the last batch of cookies in an airtight container. "There's a salad in the icebox and potatoes wrapped in foil ready for the oven in about an hour."

"Oh, Mamie, I could have done all that. You work too hard as it is."

"Don't be silly. Hard work never hurt a body. Jest look at yourself."

"Aren't you and Cotton joining us?"

She shook her head. "Square dancin' at the Community Center."

"How'd you manage to get your usually laid-back husband to go square dancing?"

"Lord a mercy, I couldn't get Cotton West on a dance floor for love ner money. He's the caller. Been doin' it for years."

She was halfway hoping Cotton and Mamie would

be around tonight to share in her idea if Ryder liked it. Or maybe she just needed a friendly face in case he didn't. "Couldn't we find two more steaks so you and Cotton could join us? You've got to eat, too."

"Ain't you sweet for thinkin' of us, but tonight's pot-luck supper. There'll be enough fried chicken and casseroles to choke a horse. I'd say y'all come with us, but the only dancin' that man a yours likes is boot scootin' and belly rubbin'."

Sam smiled sadly. If only Ryder *was* her man for real.

"Now what's that droopy grin about?"

"Oh." Sam shrugged. "Nothing."

"What? Don't think he's your man?"

Sam looked up, a little stunned that the other woman had read her mind. "I never said anything about—"

"Don't have to. It's there, plain as the nose on your face."

"Is it that obvious?" Sam asked, worried that Ryder might see the same thing.

"Only if a body's lookin'."

"Is...do you think Ryder's looking?"

Mamie thought for a moment before answering. "I reckon he's like every other man since Adam. Takes 'em a while 'fore they realize paradise ain't worth much less they got a good woman to share it. Ryder may be a mite slower than most on account of feeling he had to make good 'fore he could start searchin' for the right woman." Mamie smiled. "Reckon he never figured the right woman would jest show up on his doorstep."

Sam's heart soared. "What makes you think I might be the right woman?"

"The way he looks at you—"

"Oh, that. It's no secret he wants me physically."

"He'd be dead if he didn't. But I'm talkin' 'bout the way he looks at you when you ain't lookin'."

"Like how?"

"Well, it's more than lust, I can tell you that. And I seen him in lust enough times to know."

"You won't say anything to him, will you?"

Mamie laughed. "I won't have to. He'll figure it out for hisself. Course, it might take him a little bit. The boy's stubborn. There's no gettin' around that. But you jest hang in there."

"Thanks, Mamie."

"Welcome as sunshine, honey. Now, I got to get myself to the house. *My* man'll have a hissy fit if we're late."

A few minutes after Mamie left, Sam saw Ryder striding toward the house. He walked through the back door and straight to her. "Hello, sugar." Then he took her in his arms and kissed her.

Sam melted against him, loving his arms around her, loving him. "Hello, yourself," she said.

"Thanks for coming down to see the boys this morning. They loved the attention. Come to think of it, so did I."

"You were wonderful with them."

"Yeah." He laughed. "So good now they're pesterin' me to show them some driving techniques."

"And will you?"

"You kiddin'?" He released her, walked to the sink and began washing his hands. "You need a car with a great motor and an already beat-up body to do that. A demolition-derby car. No such beast around here."

Sam had planned on waiting until after dinner to bring up her idea, but now that an opportunity had presented itself, she decided to move ahead. "Are those kinds of cars expensive?"

Ryder shrugged. "Not really. Probably put one together for under five hundred. Like I said, the body's no big deal. Keeping the motor in prime condition is the important thing."

"But if you had such a car you've got enough room on this property for a track of some sort, don't you?"

"Yeah. Why?"

It was now or never, Sam decided. "Ryder, when you took over the ranch did you ever think about doing anything else with it but a guest ranch?"

He picked a towel from a rack on one side of the kitchen sink and dried his hands. "It was already set up and running that way when my dad died. What are you getting at, Sam?"

She took a deep breath. "A stunt school."

"A what?"

"Stunt school. The idea came to me today when I watched you with the boys. It seemed so logical that I wondered if maybe you'd had the same idea, but decided against it."

"You mean turn the ranch into a school to teach stunt work?" He looked dumbfounded.

"Yes. And not with just movies in mind. You know

that Dallas is referred to as the third coast as far as the film industry is concerned. There's the Los Colinas studio, plus production companies use Texas as location shoots constantly. But there are also stunt shows at various theme parks, locally and across the country—Disney World, Six Flags Over Texas. There's usually more than one show in each park, and there are dozens of parks. All potential work for stunt people. You've got enough land to set up a school, and you've certainly got the expertise."

"I'm ashamed to say it never crossed my mind. Don't know why, but it never did."

Adrenaline and hope spurted through Sam. "Is that something that sounds good to you? Something you might like to do?"

Ryder saw the spark of hope in her eyes and had to admit it was infectious. "Like? Try love. Try over the moon. Sam, this is a great idea. A fantastic idea."

As hopeful as she was, Sam knew she needed to show him the problems as well as the plus side. "Hold on a minute. I'm sure you realize you can't just wave a magic wand and presto change-o you go from guests to stunts. However, I've been doing some research and I think there's a possibility. Only a possibility, mind you, but—"

Ryder grabbed her in a bear hug, twirled her around the room until she was dizzy. "My smart, sexy—" he kissed her "—wonderful, Sam." He kissed her again. "You've done it. You've hit the jackpot."

"Ryder," she said, breathlessly clutching his shirt

when her feet touched the floor. "It's still just an idea. I don't want you to be disappointed if—"

"If it doesn't work, I know. But it'll work, Sam. I can feel it. And it feels right. God—" he kissed her several more times "—you're a genius." Smiling, he gazed into her eyes. "My very own beautiful genius."

As much as she thrilled being in his arms and even more being called his very own, she knew she needed to stay focused. A few more kisses and she might forget her own name, much less business details. "You might not think so after you find out what kind of hard work is involved."

Still smiling, Ryder said, "You can't scare me with hard work."

"There's a lot more to it than that. It would mean changing the ranch, your whole life. Are you prepared to do that?"

"Sam, you changed my life the day you showed up, and it's been nothing but good. You told me you were good with numbers. Sugar, you're not just good, you're the queen of numbers. Just give me everything you've got so far. We'll work it out."

"Then wait right here." Sam dashed to the office and returned with the manila envelope containing her information. Ryder pulled out chairs for them, and she spread papers out on the table. "Okay, let's get started."

For the next hour Sam bombarded Ryder with questions about stunt work. How long did he study the craft? How did he begin to get jobs? As he talked, she saw passion spark his eyes, animate his face. Obviously, he had loved what he did, and she prayed he would get the chance to do the work he loved again. The chance to hang on to his land, his heritage.

"I printed out information from three different schools," Sam told him. "What I need you to do is read them and make notes about their programs, their requirements."

"You got it."

"But all of this just scratches the surface, Ryder. I won't lie and say you can do it on a shoestring. It'll take money."

"The equipment alone will be pricey."

"And insurance."

"Can I get another loan, do you think?"

"I'm not sure, Ryder. You've got the credentials, but that may not be enough. And for a while, at least, you'll probably have to continue to court guest business until you can get the school up and running." She shuffled through the printed pages. "Here. This school in Washington State runs a sort of camp for three weeks every year. They schedule workshops practically from daylight until dark, covering a lot of areas. The fee is only for the workshops and meals, with arrangements for the clients to stay at a hotel nearby. But with the cabins you could offer a full package. Classes, meals and lodging. You could do the camp as a way to get started before trying to go full-time."

"How much money are we talking here?"

"I honestly don't know, and it's one of the reasons I hated to get your hopes up with this idea."

"No, Sam." He reached across the table and covered

her hands with his. "You saw a way out and went for it. I appreciate that, more than I can say. And no matter what the outcome, we've got to take this as far as we can."

"I'm glad you feel that way. I can put a business plan together, but a lot of the information has to come from you. Before I can go looking for money I need you to come up with a list of equipment I can price, possible improvements, alterations to the property. There's a real possibility we could find some money through government sources. We may fall under the National Endowment for the Arts, or something similar at the state level. It won't be a cinch, but I think we have a shot."

"Thanks to you."

"I told you I'd do everything I could to help."

"Yeah." Ryder looked away for a moment, then back at her. "Speaking of the deal, I know you originally thought you'd only need a week or two to delay the appraisal and reorganize things. That was the agreement, and I'll sure as hell stick to it if that's what you still want, only..." He got up from the table, walked to the counter as if not sure what to do next, then he turned and faced her. "Well, this idea of yours is good. Really good. But you're right. It's a lot of work. Too much for one person, and..." He took a deep breath. "What I'm tryin' to say, and being damned clumsy at it, is that I want you to stay, Sam. Will you?"

Her heart almost shot out of her chest until she realized he'd only talked about too much work for one person. Only work. She told herself she was insane for not sticking to their original time limit. Leaving would save some heartache, wouldn't it? But the truth was, now or later, leaving would hurt just as much.

"A deal is a deal," she said, trying to act nonchalant even though she wanted to cry.

"This isn't about the deal."

"But you just said—"

"I said I was damned clumsy, and that's sure as hell the truth." He walked to the table, squatted until he was eye level with her. "Stay with me, Sam. Deal or no deal. Please?"

If he hadn't said please maybe she could have done the sane thing. Maybe she could have walked away. No, she was lying to herself to even think walking away from him was possible. She'd been a fool for falling in love with him. What difference did it make if she was an even bigger fool for agreeing to stay?

7

RYDER COULDN'T believe how much brighter the world looked after talking with Sam the night before. The air smelled sweeter, he decided as he walked toward the corral. Come to think of it, everything was sweeter since Sam had unexpectedly dropped into his life. And he wasn't just thinking about the sex, although that was definitely mind-blowing. It might sound as if he was putting the cart before the horse, but he'd discovered that he liked Sam. Maybe not exactly a media-alerting revelation, but for Ryder, it was important. In the past he'd enjoyed women, even thought he loved a couple. He liked Sam. He liked the easy way she laughed, the way she looked a person in the eyes when she talked to them. She was smart, funny, sexy. A head for numbers and a body that was nothing short of spectacular. All the things that went into making her the kind of woman he'd just about given up on ever finding. In a nutshell, she fit him. In bed and out. He wasn't exactly sure what he was supposed to do with this particular insight, but just having it felt good. And feeling good was the order of the day. Yessir, Miss Samantha Collins might not have galloped into his life on a white horse, but damn if she hadn't arrived just in time to save the day, the ranch...and the cowboy.

Strange way to put it, but it was true. Stranger still, he hadn't even known he needed saving until Sam came along with her bright smile, sharp mind and off-the-wall deal. She was just about the best thing to happen to him since...since before Alicia. He never thought he'd say that, but it was true. And this new idea of hers was nothing short of a miracle. Whoa, he thought. Sam had warned him not to get ahead of himself, and here he was thinking about miracles. They were far from home free, and he knew it. The cloud he'd been walking on ever since she mentioned a stunt school wasn't so high he couldn't see the ground. But, dammit, for the first time in a long time, he could hold his head high and look at the future without dreading what was ahead. He couldn't wait to share his news with Cotton and Mamie.

"Well, ain't you beamin' like sunshine," Cotton said as he strolled up.

"Cotton, old friend, old buddy, old pal, you don't know the half of it," he said and slapped the cowboy on the back. "Let's you and I go find that lovely wife of yours and sweet-talk her out of a cup of her great coffee."

"You sick or somethin'?" Cotton asked as they headed toward his house.

"Never felt better."

"Sure now? 'Cause you're talkin' plumb loco."

Ryder laughed. He felt a little loco and could highly recommend it. "Nope, I just need to talk to you and Mamie. It's important."

"Can it wait a half hour? I promised a couple a the

hands I'd help 'em unload Whistler. Herb Roberts called, said he'd be bringin' him back this morning, and they're due here any minute."

"Well, sure, I guess it can wait that long. Besides, you're right. It takes at least three men to handle Whistler. Need a fourth?"

"Never hurts. That bull was born mean, and gettin' hauled around in a trailer don't improve his disposition none."

One of the hands gave a yell and pointed to a truck pulling a trailer coming up the road. As the truck braked to a halt, jarring the trailer, almost a ton of irritated bull snorted and stamped his disapproval. Herb Roberts stuck his head out the window of his truck. "Where you want him?"

"Down to the big pen on the other side of the barn," Cotton told him.

Herb took off in a cloud of dust for the pen. Ryder, Cotton and two ranch hands followed. By the time they reached the pen with an unloading chute, Herb was working on the harness that secured the bitless bridle around the bull's head to a bar on the outside of the trailer. A cumbersome thing, but necessary to keep the animal from possible injury during transport. Whistler had gone past irritation to downright mad. Cotton raised the gate on the chute while one of the cowboys opened the tailgate of the trailer to form a ramp. Ryder and the other hand picked up a couple of wooden prods hanging on the rail of the pen and prepared to assist. But Whistler wasn't in a cooperative mood.

"Watch yourself," Ryder warned the cowboy nearest him when he reached through one of the trailer's slats in an effort to keep the bull's horns from getting hung up. The bull's head was free, but he seemed not to realize he could be, too, if he'd just back up. He stood his ground, rocking his massive bulk from side to side, thrashing against the trailer, taking one step back, then one step forward. Frustration levels for men and beast rose sharply. So did bellows and profanity.

"Hardheaded sombitch," a hand yelled. "He's gonna hurt himself."

"Cost me a vet bill, will ya?" Ryder said, stepping up with the prod. He poked the bull hard, but not hard enough to cause injury. Whistler bellowed, snorted, but didn't back up.

"He's gonna tear that trailer to hell and gone," said the cowboy nearest Cotton.

"The hell he is." Cotton leaped up on the tailgate, grabbed Whistler's tail and gave a yank. Whistler moved. Still agitated and shifting his weight, instead of coming straight back, he went to one side, and his right rear hoof slipped off the ramp. He listed like a foundering ocean liner. All four men, plus Herb Roberts, sprang into action at once. Still holding his tail, Cotton moved up the ramp, trying to pull the animal up. Then, as abruptly as he'd slipped, Whistler was upright again, shifting his weight to the other side and right into Cotton, trapping him between the side wall of the trailer and nearly two thousand pounds of wild-eyed, mad-as-hell bull.

Ryder couldn't move fast enough. His arms and legs sudden felt like lead. "Cotton, get outta there," he yelled, fear clogging his throat, his heart racing like wild horses. He jumped onto the trailer, dropped his shoulder, slammed it into the bull's side. Out of the corner of his eye he saw Cotton's body slump as one of the hands pulled him out of the way and out of the trailer. With Whistler inside, Ryder scrambled down and slammed the tailgate closed.

The cowboy who had grabbed Cotton had half carried, half dragged him aside and sat him on a tree stump. He looked at Ryder. "Think he's got a couple of broken ribs."

"Get to the house. Call nine-one-one."

Kneeling beside Cotton, Ryder removed the battered old hat to see if his friend's head was damaged.

"Hey, where you goin' with my hat?" Cotton demanded.

"Just seein' if that hard head of yours wound up with any bumps." Ryder's hands were shaking.

"Hell, I just got the wind knocked outta me. Let me up." But when the sage foreman tried to stand he moaned and couldn't get a full breath.

"Where the hell do you think you're going? Sit your butt down right now."

"Don't hafta yell," he told Ryder. "Ribs is probably broke, but my ears is workin' fine."

"You're not moving a muscle until the paramedics get here and check you out. You hear me, Cotton West?"

"Hell, half the county hears you."

Finally, Ryder calmed down enough to take a full breath, and it was none too steady. The thought of losing Cotton scared him spitless. How in the world could he ever look Mamie in the eye with that kind of bad news? How in the world could he go on without the only family he had left? As the adrenaline rush finally began to subside, he felt so weak with relief he grabbed the fence rail for support. Just about then, the cowboy he'd sent to call nine-one-one came running back. Sam was with him.

She came to a screeching halt when she saw them. "Oh, my God." Her gaze flew from Cotton to Ryder and back again. "Are you both hurt?"

"You'd think he was the one on the business end of that bull the way he's yellin'." Cotton pointed to Ryder.

"Only because you're so stubborn you don't know when you're hurt."

"I told you—"

"You told me. You're always tellin' me—"

"Stop it," Sam snapped. "You're both stubborn as army mules—and white as sheets, I might add."

Having heard the bull and seen Sam and the hand running toward the barn, Mamie came out of her little house to see what all the commotion was about. Several other hands had noticed, as well, and a crowd had formed. Mamie approached the cluster of cowboys. "What in tarnation is all the ruckus—Cotton!" She rushed to him. "Oh, dear Lord."

"Oh, now. Don't go gettin' yourself all in a dither, woman. I ain't dead."

Mamie looked at Ryder, tears in her eyes. "What happened?"

Before he could answer, the other cowboys and Herb Roberts all started telling her the events at the same time. She got the most important parts. Probably broken ribs, and medical attention on the way.

While explanations were offered, Sam stepped to Ryder's side, and neither gave any notice to their automatic response to each other. She slipped her arm around his waist. He slipped his around hers. She leaned her head on his shoulder and sighed. He rubbed his cheek against her forehead. They were still standing like that five minutes later when the paramedics arrived.

"All right, folks." Two paramedics hauled a stretcher out of their medical unit, rolled it toward where Cotton sat. "Give the man some air."

As the cluster of cowboys parted and the paramedics went to work checking out the patient, Sam glanced at Ryder. The look on his face nearly broke her heart. She squeezed her hand on his waist, but he didn't notice.

In what seemed like an hour but was hardly more than a few minutes, the paramedics had examined Cotton and determined he did indeed have broken ribs and needed to go to the hospital.

"Can't you jest do whatever you hafta do here?" he asked.

"No, sir," the young paramedic said. "We have to transport you."

"Don't be ornery, Cotton. Let them do their job."

Cotton eyed his wife. "I ain't bein' ornery."

"You ain't never been anything else," she insisted. "Now, go on and get in the ambulance."

Grumbling all the way, Cotton let the paramedic help him into the ambulance, but not before he'd arranged for four of the hands to deal with Whistler, ordering them to exercise extreme caution. "I'll be right behind you," Mamie assured him.

"We all will," Sam said. As soon as the ambulance doors closed, she, Mamie and Ryder headed toward his pickup. But when he pulled the keys from his pocket, Sam held out her hand. "I think I better drive." It was a testament to how much he trusted her that he handed over the keys without protest.

Three hours later, the Lewisville hospital released a bandaged and not altogether happy patient. "Came in here with trouble breathin' and be damned if they didn't go and make it worse," he groused as Ryder helped him into the truck.

"Stop bellyachin'," Mamie said. "The doctors had to fix it so your ribs'd heal, didn't they?" Once they were all snugly wedged into the cab of the truck, she leaned forward, spoke to Ryder. "How soon you reckon those tranquilizer pills the doctor give him gonna take effect?"

"I heard that," Cotton said.

"Just wanna know how long it'll be before we don't have to listen to you complain' and..." She sighed as Cotton laid his head back on the seat and appeared to sleep. "Thank the good Lord." Mamie's voice broke on the last word, tears flowing unchecked down her cheeks. When Sam reached over and held her hand, she patted it. "I'll be fine. Jest needed a good cry and didn't wanna do it in front a him."

"I know."

"Godamighty. Scared the stuffin' outta me when I saw him sittin' on that stump, no color in his face. I couldn't imagine what had happened."

"It was my fault," Ryder said. "I should have been at the back of the trailer."

"Well, now, that's crazy. How'd you know what that bull was gonna do? Them animals is unpredictable as Texas weather. No fault of yours."

"Just the same—"

"Ryder," Mamie said, her voice stronger. "You were scared as I was. I know you love this old—" she brushed a lock of snow-white hair from Cotton's forehead "—so-and-so, as much as I do. If you'd had any notion what that bull or Cotton was gonna do, you'd a stepped in his place. So, let's have no more talk about blame. Besides, by sunup tomorrow he'll be his old self and drivin' us all crazy when he finds out he can't do anything but gripe for the next few days."

They were silent the rest of the way home. Mamie put her arm around Cotton, gently pulled his head onto her shoulder. Sam sat close to Ryder as he drove. Despite Mamie's admonition, she could see the worry on his face. And the guilt. She had to admit she was still shaky. Cotton and Mamie had become so dear to her in the short time she'd known them that the thought of anything happening to either of them made her heart sick. For all their bickering and blustering, they belonged together. They were Ryder's family. It was then that she realized, no matter what happened between her and Ryder, she would always treasure them as the family she'd never had. And leaving them would be almost as painful as leaving Ryder. Almost.

Cotton was groggy when they returned to the ranch. They got him into his bed. Ranch hands began streaming into the West house almost as soon as Ryder's truck stopped. Tom Booker must have called his wife, because Rosemary was waiting, eager to see if she could do anything to help.

"Well," Mamie said when she walked into her living room packed with friends, "he's comfortable and out, thank goodness, for a few hours."

Sighs of relief traveled around the room. "I won't say the worst is over 'cause y'all know what a pill he can be when he ain't busy."

"Yeah." Tom Booker piped up. "Reckon we'll have to hog-tie him to get him to sit still come tomorrow."

"You volunteerin', Tom?" somebody asked.

"Hell, no. I'd just as soon tackle ol' Whistler myself." And everybody laughed, reassured their friend was going to be all right.

The hands hung around for a few minutes, then gradually they returned to their work. Mamie insisted she was fine, Cotton would be fine and they could all go about their business, but with her thanks. Rosemary Booker offered to bring a meal, and Tom volunteered to take over most of Cotton's workload until he was one hundred percent again. After promising to return in a couple of hours, Sam and Ryder walked to the main house.

"What time is it?" Ryder asked when they stepped inside.

"Nearly two o'clock. We missed lunch."

He stood beside a kitchen chair, one hand on his hip, the other on the chair, his back to her. His head was down.

"Would you like me to fix you something to eat?"

When he shook his head, she crossed to him, put her hand on his shoulder. With just that touch, suddenly a ravenous, undeniable need swamped him. Memories rushed in. Hours in a hospital. Cliff. His mother. He waited for the overwhelming sense of loneliness that always accompanied the memories. But it didn't come. Not like it had in the past. Sam's touch kept it at bay. And he realized he needed her. Not her body. Not even her heart. He needed *her*. Everything she was. Everything he was when he was with her. The need was so powerful it wiped away everything else. Nothing mattered but her. He pulled her into his arms. "Sam," he whispered, just the sound of her name a comfort, a soothing balm for his aching need.

She wrapped her arms around his neck, pressed her body to his to get as close to him as possible. "I'm here. Right here."

"I...I need you."

He hadn't realized he'd said the words out loud. And until this very instant he hadn't realized the depth of his need. It scared him. The breadth and depth of it were more terrifying than his fear of losing Cotton, of losing everything. He didn't want to need her. A thought skipped through his brain that he could love her, but his emotions were too volatile for him to completely grasp the concept. Need, he understood. Love was overload. Too much, too risky, too...

"Thanks." He took a quick step back, releasing her. "Thanks for all you did. I appreciate it."

"You...you're..." The change in him was so abrupt, so startling, for a moment she felt slightly dazed. "...welcome." If she hadn't seen the change with her own eyes, she wasn't sure she would have believed it. She stared at him. One minute he'd been whispering her name, saying he needed her, and the next he was offering a polite thank-you. "Ryder—"

"I think I'll check on that damn bull," he said, taking another step away from her. "If Mamie calls..."

"Uh, yeah. I'll, uh, I'll come and find you."

"Thanks." And then he was gone.

Sam stared at the back door. What in the world had happened to make him switch from hot to cold in a heartbeat? She thought about the events of the last few minutes, then the last few hours, trying to find some reason for his behavior. But there was nothing. Nothing except him saying he needed her. Could that be it? Maybe he considered that a momentary weakness he would just as soon forget. Some people, some men, had a hard time dealing with emotion, much less expressing it. Maybe he thought of the words as a slip of the tongue he regretted. But he hadn't bothered to guard his expression when Cotton was hurt. There had been deep concern in his eyes, etched into his face for everyone to see. On the other hand, when she walked up on the scene they'd been sniping at each other. Maybe that's how Ryder handled fear.

Sam shook her head. It made her realize that for all the intimate moments they'd shared, she didn't know Ryder very well. She knew what pleased him sexually, but so far, he'd given her only glimpses of what made him tick. Maybe that was her answer. Everything that had happened today was intensely personal in a way that went past their agreement. Maybe he felt she was intruding somehow or had overstepped some boundary. No, that didn't make sense, and neither did trying to convince herself she didn't know what Ryder was like deep down inside. She'd just been witness to it.

Frustrated, she ran a hand through her hair. She could speculate all day long, and it wouldn't do any good. Only one person could answer her questions. As much as she hated to be the possible cause of any more stress than he'd experienced today, she was determined to handle the situation the only way she knew how—straightforward.

AFTER HE LEFT the house, Ryder headed for the pens near the back barn, partly to check on the bull as he'd told Sam and partly because he needed to collect his thoughts. But it wasn't that easy. He kept remembering the way Sam had looked at him when he pulled away from her. Almost like he'd hurt her. Hell, he'd been so shaken, it was a wonder he hadn't run like a spooked deer during hunting season. Maybe he owed her an apology. Probably. What did he say? *Sorry, I have intimacy issues.* Yeah, right. That sounded so pitifully clinical and corny it was laughable. Besides, he didn't have intimacy issues or any such bull. God knew he'd been more intimate with Sam than he'd been with any woman he'd ever known. The bottom line was that he was more comfortable with their relationship on a physical level. Nothing wrong with that. And no reason not to keep it that way.

"Ryder?"

He turned and found Sam a few feet away.

"Does Mamie need me?"

"No. I..." Now that she was face-to-face with him, her nerve wilted slightly. "Well, I was just wondering if I'd said or done something wrong?"

He knew where this conversation was headed, but he couldn't insult her a second time and just walk away. "No. Course not."

"You seemed...upset when you left the house, and I thought—"

"No, you didn't do anything wrong. Listen, if I was rude, I'm sorry. You were great today. I mean really great, the way you helped Mamie and stayed right with her at the hospital."

"You were there, too."

"Well, yeah, but I think a woman always feels better with another woman around at a time like that. Anyway, you were a real trooper today, and I appreciate it. Especially since we're basically strangers to you. I'm sure you didn't expect all this turmoil to be part of our deal."

Strangers? She couldn't believe he'd said that to her. She might not have known Cotton for years, but he wasn't a stranger. Neither was Mamie. And she was sick of hearing about their deal. It was so much more to her now. As soon as the thought formed, Sam realized she had her answer. Just because it was more to her didn't mean he felt the same. "No, I guess I didn't."

He smiled. "Don't worry. Cotton's gonna be right as rain, and everything will be back to normal by tomorrow. Besides, you and I have got a lot of work to do if we're gonna plan for the stunt school."

Business as usual, she thought. A deal is a deal. She should be happy to have everything back to normal, shouldn't she? Sure, she should. It made things easier, simpler. Then why did she feel like crying? Why did she feel as if something precious had suddenly slipped from her grasp? "The school. Right. In all the commotion I nearly forgot about it."

"You know, I didn't even get the chance to tell Cotton your ideas."

She didn't know what to say, only that at this moment she wanted to be away from him. "Well, uh, I'll be interested to hear what he thinks. Uh, I'm going back to the house, maybe grab a sandwich. Sure I couldn't make one for you?"

"Thanks. I'm good."

She nodded. "See you later, then."

"Yeah."

Ryder watched her walk away and had to fight the urge to call after her and apologize for his apology. He'd hurt her again, and that truly was the last thing he wanted.

Sam didn't look back, but went straight to the office and kept herself busy for the rest of the day. It was the only way she could keep from dwelling on her conversation with Ryder. And if she dwelled on the conversation... Well, it was best not to. He'd made it clear he wasn't interested in anything but their physical arrangement. So be it. Just because she was in love with him didn't mean she could expect happily ever after. She knew that. If she'd forgotten it, if she'd let herself get too wrapped up in romance, Ryder had certainly set her straight this afternoon. He couldn't have been more clear if he'd said, "Back off." So that's what she would do.

And then what?

Could she hold to their deal, loving him as she did, knowing it was strictly one-sided? She always had the option to leave. Simple enough. Just tell him it wasn't working, the ranch was hopeless, and leave. But that wasn't true. The ranch wasn't hopeless. And she didn't want to leave. She'd gone into this situation with her eyes open, and there was no reason to cry foul now. The only promise Ryder had made her was for dazzling sex, and he'd certainly kept it. She'd had enough disappointments in her life not to expect them, deal with them. After all, she was good at facing reality. And the reality was, she loved Ryder, but he didn't love her back. He wanted their deal, nothing more. Maybe another woman would have walked, but Sam knew there was little enough fun and affection in this world. If that's all she could have, she'd take it.

"DANG, WOMAN. I don't need no blanket."

"You've got a temperature," Mamie said.

Sam, who'd just stepped in to see Cotton, watched the exchange, barely containing a grin.

"I'm gonna have a heat stroke sure as hell if you keep flingin' this damn—" He glanced at Sam. "Pardon my French, will ya, Sam?"

She nodded and let her smile break free. "I see you're feeling better."

"Thought we'd have some peace and quiet, but no," Mamie said. "As you see, he's up and ornery, jest like I predicted."

"Would you really want him any other way?" Sam winked at Cotton.

Mamie sighed. "I'm goin' to get you some soup," she told her husband. "Sam's come to visit. Be nice. And no ranch talk."

"Nice," he grumbled. "Jest 'cause I took a nap in the middle of the day, she's treatin' me like an invalid. It's almost dark. I figured Ryder would a come by now."

"He's, uh... The last time I saw him he was going to check on the bull—"

"Damn clumsy son of a bitch. Oughta shoot 'im, if he wasn't the best damn breeder in these parts." He rubbed his rib cage. "You know if them cowboys got that section of fence repaired over by the Shetland Arena?"

"You're not supposed to be asking about work. You're supposed to be resting."

"I broke my ribs, not my head. I'll be back out there come sunup tomorrow."

"Ryder insisted you take at least another day."

"He may think he runs this place, but I got news for

him." Cotton looked straight into Sam's eyes, a worried look on his face. "He all right?"

"He was worried about you, but we all were."

"No, I mean, he didn't..."

"Didn't what?"

He studied her for a moment as if trying to decide how to answer, or as if deciding he'd said too much. "He ever say anything 'bout his family?"

"He told me about Cliff, and his mother, and—"

"Well, then." Cotton heaved a sigh of relief. "Since he told you that much, don't feel like I'm talkin' outta turn to ask if he sorta, like the kids say, 'flipped out'? I thought maybe the thing with the bull might remind him of Cliff."

"Oh," Sam said, the light dawning. "Oh, Cotton, I never thought about that."

"Yeah, well. He don't talk about it much, but I know it preys on his mind from time to time."

"He was a little distant," she said, thrilled to be able to pinpoint a reason for his behavior. One that had nothing to do with her, at least. Now, his coolness made more sense.

"Went off by himself, didn't he?" Sam nodded. "Yep. He'll come outta it, though. Ain't one to waller round feeling sorry for hisself."

"No, I don't think he is."

"No, sirree, Bob. Not when he's got the ranch to consider. It's too important. And I know things is rough, but he ain't gonna give up till they carry him outta here feet first." Cotton gave a nod as though to say, "So there." "Not that I reckon that'll happen with you hel-pin' him." He leaned forward, lowered his voice. "Ain't really none of my bizness, but how y'all doin'?"

"We're..." She didn't feel comfortable saying anything about the stunt school idea until Ryder had talked to Cotton and Mamie. "Working on it."

He sat back. "My money's on Ryder. And you," he added.

"Thanks. I have to admit there's a lot more to running a ranch of any kind than I ever dreamed."

"It's hard work, but them that love it wouldn't do nothin' else. Some come to it natural. Cliff did from the first breath he drew. It took Ryder a while, but he come to it all by hisself. And I tell you, what he feels for this place is jest as deep, jest as wide, as what Cliff felt. Maybe more 'cause he fought it for so long. But you could see it in his eyes when he come for his daddy's funeral. There jest wasn't no place else on earth he wanted to be. Why, if he lost this ranch I think he'd wither away to nothin'. Or worse. Maybe go back to doin' them dangerous stunts till he let one of 'em kill him."

"Oh...no."

"Sounds a mite harsh, don't it? I reckon it's hard for city folks like yourself to understand how we feel about our land. It's life to ranchers, farmers and the like. It's what makes us keep hopin'."

"I understand better than you think, Cotton. I've worked for over five years to pay off five acres of land. It's the only thing that's ever been mine alone, and when I walk across it, wander through the trees, I feel like I'm in another world—some place very special, and I'm connected to it. Someday I'll build my dream house on that land. Live there, dream there."

"You got it. You understand right enough, and—"

There was a knock at the door. "I'll get it," Sam offered. When she opened the door, there stood Ryder with a dish of food in his hands.

"C'mon in," Cotton said. Mamie came into the room as Ryder stepped inside and Sam closed the door.

"I ran into Tom Booker on my way over. His missus sent this." He handed the dish to Mamie. "She said you could freeze it."

"Well, ain't that sweet a her. Sit down. You had supper? Just soup, but—"

"No, thanks, Mamie, but since we're all here I would like to talk to you, if you're feeling up to it, Cotton."

"Hellfire, don't you start, too. I'm fine as frog hair." Mamie rolled her eyes.

Ryder grinned. "All right, then. Let's all sit, and I'll tell you the idea Sam came up with. I think it's the answer to our problems."

For the next hour and a half, including moving the discussion to the dinner table for soup and homemade bread, the four of them discussed the idea. Mamie and Cotton had some of the same questions Sam and Ryder had voiced and some new ones.

"Who's gonna do all this teachin'?" Cotton wanted to know. "You can't do it all."

"What hands we have can do a lot. All of them can teach basic horseback riding. Most have rodeoed. At least two come to mind that I could teach to work with horse stunts. I know that last man we hired does mo-

tocross on weekends. And, believe me, I know enough
people in the business who would jump at the opportunity to do this kinda of work *and* draw a steady paycheck. I don't think I'll have any trouble findin' instruc-
tors."

After wrangling over the ins and outs and what ifs,
everyone agreed that the idea was solid and workable,
but the biggest stumbling block was the money. "And
Sam's working on that," Ryder said. "You understand," he told Mamie and Cotton. "None of this may
work out, but at least it's a chance, and a good one. But
I can't do it without you two. And I need to know how
you honestly feel about all of this."

Cotton opened his mouth to speak, but Mamie's
hand on his silenced him. "You don't even have to ask.
As long as you're happy, we're happy." She looked at
her husband. They smiled at each other. "We're with
you, no matter what."

"Damn straight," Cotton said.

After the dishes were cleaned up, Ryder and Sam
headed to the main house. Ryder flopped down on the
sofa in the living room. "It's been a hell of a day."

Sam laughed and dropped down beside him. "I
think that qualifies as the understatement of the day.
Maybe the decade."

"But old Cotton sure got sparked, didn't he? He's
champin' at the bit to get moving on our plan."

"I don't know how much champin' Mamie will al-
low with those broken ribs."

"Aw, they'll heal quick enough. I've been there a few
times myself."

"A lot?"

"What?"

"Did you have a lot of injuries when you were in the stunt business?"

"My fair share, I guess. Broken ribs, collarbone, my nose, twice. I separated a shoulder once hanging from a helicopter. And I got this." He pulled his collar aside to indicate the scar she'd wondered about the first night they made love.

"What happened?"

"A fake bar fight. This other stuntman and I were struggling. He pulled a knife, went for my throat, just like we rehearsed, but—" he shrugged "—just one of those quirky things. Two other guys were fighting next to us. One lost his balance and fell, hitting my partner's elbow. Thank goodness the knife wasn't real or it would have gone deep."

When she reached up and gently ran her fingertips along the jagged line on the ridge of his collarbone, he captured her hand, held it. "That just made it all worthwhile."

It felt like the most natural thing in the world for her to put her lips to that very spot. And just as natural to keep going until she reached his mouth.

Her kiss was like coming home. However he'd hurt her earlier, she'd forgiven him with a sweet homecoming. The tension of the day melted from him, replaced by another brand of tension. One he knew how to relieve. "We never did take that sunset walk," he said when the kiss ended.

"At the risk of repeating myself, there will be another sunset tomorrow."

"So, forget the walk?"

"Walk me to the bedroom," she said.

8

"Awesome," Sam whispered.

As usual Ryder had woken before the alarm sounded, then he'd kissed her awake and they'd made slow, sweet love. Now facing each other, he absently toyed with a lock of her hair while she looked over his shoulder at the sunrise.

"Thanks."

"I was referring to the sunrise," she said.

"Oh." He faked a stab to his heart and fell back onto the pillow. "Wounded. Mortally wounded."

"Your ego can withstand a direct hit."

"Yeah?"

"Absolutely, and you've got a cast-iron will to go along with it."

"I hope you're right." With a sigh he drew her close. "I'm gonna need all of it today." Playfulness vanished, and she knew he was referring to his appointment that afternoon with the vice president of the bank to present the reorganization plan for the ranch and another request for an extension. Sam put her hand on his chest, felt his heartbeat beneath her fingertips and thought how much she loved him, how desperately she wanted him to be happy. And his happiness was all tied up in Copper Canyon Ranch. "You'll do fine."

"I have to. This is my last chance, Sam."

Over the past four days they had worked practically nonstop, taking all of Sam's research and constructing a detailed business plan that would, they hoped, knock the socks off the bankers. Ryder had pulled together everything of value he still owned—stocks, bonds, some pasture land in Denton and, most important, oil leases that had been a source of income for the Wells family for over forty years. Most of it had already been liquidated, with the exception of the leases, which were in the hands of a broker and expected to sell. It would be enough to cover the overdue payments, but it would be for nothing if an extension wasn't granted.

Ryder had done something he'd never thought he could do. He'd gone to several contacts he still had in the film business in California and asked for references to include in the presentation. Asking for those references had been a dose of humility. But Sam had worked her guts out on this proposal. It was the least he could do.

Ryder turned to her. "In case I haven't said it lately, I'm grateful for everything you've done. None of this would be happening if it weren't for you."

"Thanks, but we're not home free yet. Even with the payments up to date, they could decide to be hard-nosed and—"

"You sound as if you expect them to reject the extension."

"Oh, Ryder, I'm sorry. I didn't mean to sound like gloom and doom. In fact, I don't expect them to turn you down. You've covered the back payments, reorganized and have a wonderful business plan that shows great potential, so..." She smiled. "Forgive me. That was a little projection on my part."

"Projection?"

"Projecting my insecurities onto you. It's automatic. I was raised to think and act conservatively. Never think too much of myself. Always put others first. Grin and bear it, don't complain. Save, don't borrow. Why do you think I became a number cruncher and went into business management instead of something more daring like—"

"Rodeo barrel racing?"

"Exactly."

He turned so that their bodies aligned breasts to chest, hip to hip, sex to sex. "Could've fooled me. The day you showed up on my doorstep I thought you were pretty damned gutsy."

"You did not. You thought I was a deranged female."

"Yeah, but a very sexy deranged female with a hell of a proposition."

"Proposition?"

"Deal."

"That's more like it." She looked at him, a sly smile on her lips. "So you thought I was sexy, huh?"

"Still do." He palmed her breast, then slowly rubbed his thumb back and forth across her nipple. She shivered. "See what I mean? The way you respond is just about the sexiest thing I've ever seen."

"I feel..."

"What?"

She shook her head. "I'm not sure I can explain it, but something happens when you touch me. It's like... I've never been struck by lightning, but that's what it must feel like. A kind of sexual lightning. Sometimes I think I can actually feel heat shooting through my blood, along every nerve ending, every cell. And it happens every time. We—" she stopped herself before saying "made love." "Had sex not an hour ago, and it was wonderful. Slow and wonderful. Now you just touched me and..."

She gasped when he ran his hand down her back, cupped her fanny and pressed her to his arousal. "And?"

"And I can't remember anything when you do that."

"Do what? This?" Slowly, deliberately, he rocked against her. "Or this?" He leaned down, took her nipple in his mouth and sucked.

She gasped again, this time arching her back, her entire body suddenly vibrating. "I want you again."

She was right about the lightning. And suddenly the heat was overwhelming. Nothing mattered but the wanting. And more wanting. When she put her hands in his hair and pulled his head up for hungry, greedy kisses, he could have easily met her demand, but he held back, refused to be hurried. He waged a war between slow and easy and right now. They'd had a leisurely, blissful joining before, and he wanted that again. He wanted to feel her melt beneath him in a puddle of need, then to enjoy her slow, steady climb back to the heat, back to the moment when she began to shudder, moan and dissolve with satisfaction. At the same time, he wanted her as he always did, hot, quick and deep. He wanted to give her, to give them both, the tormented pleasure of slow and easy, but when she went wild with one touch it was hard not to do the same. In an effort to slow things down he slipped his tongue between her parted lips but didn't fully kiss her. Still determined not to be rushed, he withdrew and nibbled on her bottom lip for what seemed like hours before going back for another soft, hot kiss.

"Ryder." Eyes clouded with passion, her hand closed around him, guided him where she wanted him.

He almost lost control. "Easy, darlin'," he whispered against her mouth.

"No. Please."

"Sam—"

"You're trying to be gentle." Her eyes were clear, dark with hunger. "Don't."

She took his breath away. What was left of his control snapped. He quickly sheathed himself with a condom and plunged deep.

The first climax slammed into her, leaving her senseless, dizzy as a punch-drunk prizefighter. But not so senseless she wasn't ready for another round. She clung to him, met him stroke for stroke.

He'd never seen her like this. Wild, demanding, almost combative. She was a wildcat in heat, claiming her mate. Realizing she needed more, needed it all, he decided to give her full rein. He scooped his hands beneath her fanny, held her tight and rolled onto his back. From somewhere deep inside himself he found one last scrap of restraint and let her have her wild way. But it wasn't long before the restraint was gone. Then he put his hands on her hips, repositioned her slightly and began to pump his hips, surging into her, one powerful thrust after another until she arched her spine, threw back her head and cried out her satisfaction in a long, deep-throated moan. Finally, every muscle strained, every nerve taut, with one final, upward thrust he exploded in his own mind-shattering climax.

Seconds later she collapsed against him, and he rolled them onto their sides. Totally spent, they lay together until their breathing returned to normal, their bodies calmed.

Finally, Sam raised a weak hand to his chest. "I know we decided it wasn't a good idea for me to go with you to the bank, but how would you feel about me driving in with you and waiting? If I can find the strength, that is."

Ryder grinned, feeling satisfied in ways that had nothing to do with what had happened moments ago. Having her beside him emotionally as well as physically gave him a satisfaction he'd never known.

"I've got a better idea. How far is your apartment from the bank?"

"Fifteen-minute drive."

"Instead of waiting for me, why don't you swing by there and pick up your fanciest dress, shoes, the works? Just in case we have reason to celebrate."

"Hmm, great idea. And we will. I can feel it."

"I sure hope you're right."

"None of that hope stuff. Think positive. Of course,

I'm right. This is going to be big. You'll have tons of employees and megatons of satisfied graduates. Why, in the not-too-distant future the name Copper Canyon Ranch will stand for the best-trained stuntmen and women in the business. Stunt coordinators will dedicate their Oscars to you and the school."

"Whoa, sugar. Aren't you getting a little ahead of yourself?"

"Maybe," she admitted. "But it doesn't hurt to dream. And if you're going to dream, might as well dream big."

"Hold that thought, sugar."

She gave him a quick kiss then glanced at the clock beside the bed. "Uh-oh, I better jump in the shower. We've still got things to do before we leave." She climbed out of bed and started toward the bathroom.

"By the way..."

She stopped at the door, turned. "Yes?"

"You'd make one hell of a barrel racer."

She smiled, blew him a kiss, then closed the door.

Ryder sighed, as content as he could ever remember. Sexual lightning, Sam had called it, and she was right. Sometimes, it didn't even take a touch to set off the lightning. Sometimes just a glance from her was all it took to set him on fire. He'd never wanted a woman the way he wanted Sam. Not with the same depth and intensity. But then, he'd never met a woman like Sam. At first, that intensity scared him. He didn't mind admitting it had taken him a while to know how to handle the situation. Now making love with her felt like the most natural thing in the world. The most right thing in the world.

Making love? Is that what they were doing?

Without even a heartbeat of hesitation, the answer came. Yes. A terrifying yes. He took a deep breath. All right, he could admit that. And he could admit that he cared about her. They had fun together, and Lord knew they worked well together. She had a generous spirit and a loving heart, but that didn't mean he was hopelessly in love. Love didn't figure in his plans. Not now, anyway. It couldn't. Not with the loan hanging over his head.

He propped himself up on one elbow, listening to her hum in the shower. Still, if he ever did decide to really give love a try, it would probably be with a woman very much like Sam. A woman who made him laugh, who loved the ranch and his family. Someone as warm and giving. Not to mention sexy as all get out. She was one hot number, all right. In more ways than one.

Grinning from ear to ear, Ryder flopped onto the pillow. Sam was that and a box of chocolates, for sure. And damned if he wasn't one lucky man.

He only hoped his luck would hold.

THE BUTTERFLIES in Sam's stomach had gone berserk almost since they left Lewisville. As Ryder snaked in and out of traffic on Central Expressway forty-five minutes later, she kept telling herself not to worry. He would get the extension, and everything would be fine. But the butterflies weren't listening. She could tell Ryder was nervous, too. His knuckles were white as he gripped the steering wheel of the truck, and he'd stopped trying to make small talk. There was little point in talking about what might happen if he didn't get the extension. They both knew it would mean the end of Copper Canyon Ranch.

Ryder took the Park Lane exit, crossed over Central Expressway, then turned into the parking lot of the building housing the Frontier Financial Bank offices.

"We're a few minutes early," he said.

Sam smiled. "Enough to look punctual but not enough to look overeager."

He got out of the truck and she slid to the driver's seat. "Don't forget that dress," he told her, his hand resting against the door.

"I won't. And Ryder..." She leaned over and lightly kissed him on the mouth. "That's for luck."

"Thanks."

As she watched him walk up the steps and into the bank building she prayed all the luck in the world was with him.

She put the car in drive and ten minutes later parked in her assigned spot. Once inside her apartment, she locked the door behind her, dropped her keys on a table as she turned, then stopped short. Something wasn't right. She glanced around, but everything appeared to be in order. Still, she felt odd, even uncomfortable. As if she'd just walked into a stranger's home. But that was ridiculous. This was her place, her furniture, her art on the walls. She dismissed the sensation, telling herself it was only because she'd been away for a few days. But she hadn't been gone any longer than if she had taken a vacation. So why did the apartment seem so cold, so unwelcoming? Where was the sense of security she had always enjoyed? The feeling of belonging?

And then she realized why everything felt so strange. Her apartment didn't fit her anymore. *She* didn't fit here anymore. She belonged miles away on a ranch just outside Lewisville, Texas. She belonged with Ryder. In his home.

Sam sat on the closest chair. She had admitted to herself that she loved him the night they played strip poker. So loving him wasn't exactly a news flash. It wasn't just that she loved him, but what loving him had done. It had changed her in a way she hadn't anticipated.

Her home felt different because *she* was different.

She looked around her living room, the white walls, neutral colors, subtle textures and Art Deco style. The only real spark of life existed in the tastefully framed Georgia O'Keeffe prints over her fireplace and dining room table. It was all very sleek, very modern, uncluttered and...

Cold.

She hadn't realized, until this moment, how cold. She'd seen a picture in a copy of *Architectural Digest* and set out to duplicate its style, thinking that was how she wanted her life to be, clean lines, uncluttered. Well, she'd certainly accomplished that. There wasn't a ruffle or a floral print within a mile of this place. There wasn't a rustic anything to be had unless she consid-

the perpetually leaking pipe under the bathroom

sink. But most of all there wasn't any genuine warmth. The truly scary thing was that she might have lived her life this way for who knows how long if her car hadn't conked out on her at just the right moment in just the right place. Or if she hadn't lost her job, or if Ryder hadn't been in trouble. A hundred ifs. A thousand. Yet two things stood out clearly as right and true. She loved Ryder. Desperately, hopelessly. No matter what happened. Even if he didn't love her back, she knew love was possible. And she had found a part of herself she hadn't even realized was missing. She wanted what everyone wanted. To love and be loved.

Walking into her uncluttered, almost sterile apartment had been like walking into a dark space, and suddenly someone had flipped on a light. A glaring light. And what she saw no longer reflected who she was or what she wanted out of life. What she wanted, needed was Ryder, family and the ranch. In that order. But would she ever have what she needed? Their time together was growing short. They both knew it, yet neither had talked about it. She couldn't bear the thought of him saying goodbye. Not today, not next week. Not ever. If she could just stay for a while. Be with him without their deal. He'd asked her to stay for a few extra days, and she wanted a lifetime. She wanted to live with him, love him, work beside him....

There was her answer.

If—no, *when* he got the extension there would be tons of work to get the stunt school up and running. He would need help. He would still need her. Why hadn't

she thought of this before? He needed help, and she
needed a job.

But what if he didn't want her to stay on? What if
he'd be relieved to see their deal die a natural death?
Or worse, what if he asked her to stay but only to work
with him. Would she?

A few weeks ago the old, needy Sam might have
said yes, but not now, not today, she realized. The old
Sam had never truly experienced love. How could she
have known that it wasn't being loved but loving that
made all the difference? If she lost Ryder, her heart
would break. And yes, there would be pain—probably
more than she was capable of imagining at this moment. But no matter what happened she felt whole,
complete, for the first time in her life. She was her own
person. Not just a pitiful little orphan girl or a struggling career woman fighting for a rung on the corporate ladder or even a woman in love. She was all those
things and more. And she wanted to share all of herself
with Ryder. She just hoped she'd have the chance.

STANDING in the lobby of the office building waiting
for Sam to pick him up, Ryder stared out the bank of
windows mentally replaying the meeting he'd just left.
The two men, one a loan officer, the other a vice president, had listened to his proposal and, outwardly at
least, had appeared to accept it. They had asked perti-
nent questions, all of which he'd been able to answer to
their satisfaction. But he couldn't help but wonder how
much, if any, of that satisfaction would translate into
~~oval.~~ They had told him they would exam-

ine the proposal in depth, confer with their underwriters and give him an answer before the end of the week. Three short days. Maybe that was good. Maybe they thought the proposal was so workable they didn't need a lot of time to decide. Or maybe that was all the time they needed to process a rejection. But he didn't think so. In fact, his gut feeling told him the answer would be yes. Either way, in three days his life would change. But for better or worse?

After almost a year of carrying around the anxiety of possibly losing his land, his heritage, for the first time he had a real shot at not only hanging on, but making it a success the way he'd always wanted. He should have felt elated, excited, not to mention relieved. Instead he was terrified. Today, sitting in that meeting talking about his plans for the future, he realized that future didn't mean much unless Sam was a part of it. He'd been dumb as a post not to have seen it before, even dumber to have denied it.

He was in love with her.

What a liar he'd been, telling himself that if he ever decided to give love a try, it would probably be with a woman like Sam. How blind could a man be? There was no other woman like Sam. Thinking back, he knew when he'd fallen in love with her—the day Cotton had been hurt. He'd known it, but like a fool he hadn't had the courage to face it. So what had he done? Acted like the fool he was, telling her how much he appreciated her, offering her thanks. What a jackass. The ideal woman drops into his lap, and he doesn't have the sense to recognize a gem when he sees one.

And she was a gem. She was funny, sexy and smart. He loved the way she laughed, the way she walked. She was warm, generous and caring. He loved the way she was with Cotton and Mamie. He loved everything about her.

And he trusted her.

There was a time when he didn't think he'd find a woman worth trusting, but Sam had changed that. The question was, how did she feel about him?

True, she'd given her heart and soul every time they had made love, but that didn't mean she was in love. Not once had she ever led him to believe, by word or deed, that she wanted anything other than their just-sex deal. Well, maybe in deed. But just sex was supposed to be the man's approach, not the woman's. No promises, no commitments was supposed to be exactly how a man wanted a relationship. Women wanted stability. Yet the closest Sam had come to even sounding like she had anything more in mind was using phrases like "we're not home free yet." Maybe she would be glad to put this little interlude behind her and move on with her life.

Then again, maybe he was expecting too much, too quickly. Sam hadn't grown up surrounded by a loving family and friends. And by her own admission her past relationships had left something to be desired. His ego wasn't so grand that he expected every woman who came to his bed to fall for him, but he was experienced enough to know most women didn't respond the way Sam did. Most women didn't give themselves freely, totally, unless they felt something. And Sam gave herself freely and totally every time. Every instinct he had told him it was more than just sex for her. Hadn't she stayed when he asked her? Hadn't she involved herself in his life, his work? Again, his instincts told him that had to count for something. Maybe she didn't love him yet. But he would stake his life on the fact that she would in time. After all, he wasn't exactly on solid ground with loving her yet himself. But he knew it was true. For all the times he'd protested to the contrary and done everything he could to avoid love, he knew this was real. The forever kind of real.

He didn't have to stretch his imagination far to think about the two of them together, working side by side to build a life, loving each other, maybe even raising some kids. He'd worked so hard since his dad died that he hadn't allowed himself the luxury of such a dream. But it had always been there in the back of his mind. In his heart. Sam had brought it to life. He couldn't let her walk away. He had to find a way to keep her close. To give him enough time to make her see that they were right for each other. But how did he go from a deal for mutual benefit to the deal of a lifetime? The simplest, most direct route was to come right out and tell her he loved her, that he wanted her to marry him. But he wasn't sure she'd believe him. In fact, he decided, she wouldn't. And why should she? Except for asking her to stay a few days longer than originally agreed, he'd never said he wanted more than what they had. Never even hinted. And now to start talking marriage and follow it with talking about working side by side, she might think his interest was more financial than romantic. Ryder tried to put himself in her shoes. What would he think if the situation was reversed? How would he feel?

He'd think she only wanted to hang on to a damned good business manager. And he'd feel cheated.

So would Sam.

So what did he do now? He wanted her in his life permanently but he couldn't go rushing in like a bull in a china shop. Sam wasn't some calf that could be roped and hog-tied. She had to be coaxed, won. And he had to be careful or he'd blow the whole thing.

Maybe he should change the order of things. Offer her the job first, then propose later, after he'd had a chance to win her. That way she wouldn't think he wanted just a worker, not a wife. The idea might not be the straightest path between two points, but damned if he could see any other way at the moment. He would tell her when the stunt school started to take shape he would need some kind of office manager and that she was the ideal person to keep things organized and keep an eye on the budget. She certainly knew his financial situation inside and out, not to mention that she had come up with the idea for the stunt school, done most of the research and helped put the proposal together. Whatever success Copper Canyon Stunt School might achieve would be due, in no small measure, to her. For the first time in his life Ryder felt like he really had a future enough to offer the woman he loved. The important thing was that he wanted her to say yes because he wanted her to stay, and he had to make sure she understood that. He would beg her to take the job if he had to.

And what if she turned him down?

He couldn't accept that. Somehow, he would convince her to stay. He had to. And while he hated to manipulate her into staying, the truth was he needed her. Desperately. She was the most important person in his life. He couldn't let her just walk away. Tonight he would wine and dine her and ask her to stay for real. It was a risky roll of the dice, and he was betting heavily on his instincts. He watched his truck pull up to the office building. In fact, he thought, he was betting everything he had.

"I'm almost afraid to ask how it went," she said, when she slid across the seat so he could drive.

"Good. I think." He grinned. "Hell, I don't know. I'm still shaking."

"Did they like the proposal?"

"Yeah, I think they did. At least they acted like they did." He sighed, feeling some of the tension drain away. "They asked a lot of questions and seemed to be satisfied with my answers. Only, uh, negative thing they said was that it was a lot of money under the circumstances. Come to think of it, that seemed to be their biggest concern. But I reminded them there was no padding. All the expenditures were bare minimum." Suddenly, he turned in the seat, pulled her to him and kissed her hard. "God, I'm glad you're here. Knowing you were made the whole thing a lot easier."

"I, uh, I had my fingers crossed," Sam replied, startled by the emotion she could read in his face. She had seen this intensity in his eyes before, usually connected to passion, but this was something different. Deeper. She felt more connected to him than ever before. "Did they, uh, say when they would notify you?"

"Three days. They're gonna review the proposal and let me know in three days."

"That's fast."

"You think so?"

"Absolutely. I've seen loan applications take weeks before approval. They must think it looks viable. Either that or..."

"Yeah," Ryder said, when he saw the concern in her eyes. "It's the *or* that'll keep me awake tonight."

She put her hand on his arm. "I told you this morning. You've got to think positive. I know that sounds naive, but I really believe positive vibes bring positive results. So just hang on to the good thoughts, okay?"

He touched her cheek. "I don't know what I'd do without you, Sam. By the way, did you get that dress?"

"Y-yes."

"Good. 'Cause I feel like a drink and a thick steak, in that order. How about we go home, clean up and go out on the town?"

"Sounds wonderful."

Everything sounded wonderful, Sam thought, especially Ryder saying he didn't know what he'd do without her.

TWO HOURS LATER they were seated at a table for two on the patio of La Hacienda Ranch in Frisco, Texas, not far from Lewisville. The rustic restaurant had a reputation for good beef and great atmosphere. Sam ordered the sautéed trout and Ryder the biggest steak she'd ever seen. He also ordered a margarita for himself, but she declined.

"Wanna sip of my margarita?"

Sam eyed the glass for a moment. "Okay, just a sip." But one taste and she wrinkled her nose. "I'll stick with iced tea," she said.

"In case I haven't mentioned it before, you look gorgeous," he told her. "I sure like that dress." The truth was he'd nearly dropped his teeth when she walked into the kitchen and announced she was ready. One look at her in that dress, hardly more than a formfitting slip with thin little straps, and he was ready, all right— and he didn't mean ready to go out. It accentuated every curve and line of her delectable body and reminded him of how much he wanted her. And that reminded him to cool his jets. This was a time to be sincere, not sex-crazed. He had to make her feel comfortable with the idea of the two of them together for a long time before he could hope for happily ever after.

"Thanks. It was an impulse purchase a couple of months ago. To be honest, I haven't had the nerve to wear it, and I almost changed my mind tonight."

"Why?"

"Mamie said it was dangerous."

"It is. To every male over the age of twelve." At that moment a family with three young boys filed past on their way to the far end of the patio. The middle boy, probably no more than seven or eight, looked at Sam, almost tripping over his own feet. Ryder grinned. "Make that over the age of eight."

"Such sweet talk."

"You deserve it, and a lot more."

"Now you're going to make me blush."

The smile faded, and he sighed. "I'm trying to pay you a compliment and not doing too well. And this is all going to sound like I'm trying to soften you up. And I am, sorta."

"Now you've got me curious."

"It's, uh...just that I've been thinking about us...our deal."

"What about it?"

"I know it all started out as fun and games, but—"

Her heart almost skipped a beat. "You, uh..." She picked up her glass of iced tea, more to keep her trembling hands steady than out of thirst. "You don't think it's fun anymore?"

"No! It's not that," he rushed to assure her. "But I... Well, I was wondering if you've ever given thought to changing it?"

The glass halfway to her mouth, Sam stopped, set it on the table. She was sure her heart skipped a beat. Stay calm, she told herself. *Changing* could mean anything. Or everything. "I'm not sure I understand your meaning."

"The deal started out as just... Well, you know what it started out as. Two weeks ago I was so low I needed stilts to go eyeball to eyeball with a snake, and now I've got a good shot at a fresh start. All thanks to you."

"That was the—"

"Yeah, I know. What I'm trying to say is, have you thought about what you'll do afterward?"

So, this was the end, she thought. She put both hands around her glass to keep them from shaking again. Oh, please don't let this be goodbye. She didn't want it be. "A little," she lied. She dreaded hearing him talk about the end of their time together. The end of her hopes. But short of throwing herself into his arms and begging him to let her stay, how could she prevent it? Then again, what was wrong with throwing herself into his arms?

"You have to get a job, of course," he said, trying to work up to asking her to stay. He was so nervous he couldn't look her in the eyes.

"Yes. And since you mentioned it—"

"Of course, you're so smart you could do anything you wanted."

"Thank you, but—"

"I mean, if you found a job you really liked, salary might not even be your biggest concern, right?"

"Well—"

"Even, say, if it was starting at the bottom, so to speak?"

Suddenly she realized they were both dancing around the same subject. "Like with a new business? A stunt school, for instance?"

"Exactly. And I was thinking..." Ryder looked at her, barely able to draw a full breath for fear he had misunderstood her question. "Sam?"

"Yes?"

"Did you just... I've got no right to ask you to give

up the lifestyle you had in Dallas, but I'm gonna ask it anyway. Would you work with me, Sam? Would you help me get this company on its feet? I couldn't pay you much—"

"I don't care."

"—at first anyway, but maybe we could figure out some kind of—"

"Ryder."

"—bonus plan where you could eventually—"

"Ryder."

"What?"

"The answer is yes."

"Yes?"

"Yes. If you hadn't offered, I was going to ask you for the job. I want to stay and work with you. I want to be a part of what you're building." *And a part of your life,* she wanted to add.

Ryder closed his eyes for a second. "Thank God." Instinctively, he reached across the table and covered her hand with his. "I don't know what I would've done if you'd said no. You won't regret this. I promise."

Sam looked into his eyes and knew she might regret a lot of things, but loving him would never be one of them.

THE NEXT TWO DAYS were some of the happiest in Sam's memory. During the day she and Ryder worked hard, moving forward with plans for the school. And at night... There were no words to describe the nights. Everything had changed. It was probably her imagination, but even the way he touched her felt different.

Their lovemaking was sweeter, more satisfying and, if possible, more passionate that ever. It was like living a dream, and her happiness must have been evident, because even Cotton commented on it.

"You look bright as a new penny," he told her on the morning of the third day. "Don't she, wife?"

"Downright sparklin'."

"Thank you both. I feel sparkling."

"Jest wantcha to know we're keepin' our fingers crossed," Mamie said.

Sam held up both hands, fingers crossed. "Me, too."

"Gonna be nerve rackin' till that phone rings with the news."

"I know. I don't think Ryder could stand the thought of waiting around here for it to ring. He didn't sleep very well last night, and I noticed he found the most physical thing he could do today."

"I seen him down at the barn groomin' the horses right after sunup."

"Didn't eat no breakfast, neither," Mamie said. "Reckon he was jest too nervous."

Cotton poured himself a cup of coffee. "You figure this is really gonna happen, Sam?"

"Oh, I hope so. I pray it will."

"Yeah, we been doin' our fair share of that, too. What worries me is what'll happen to Ryder if it don't."

Sam's gaze went from Cotton to Mamie. "I don't even want to think about it."

"I ain't talkin' 'bout jest losin' the land. I'm talkin'

about Ryder. He's done got all his hopes up again, and this time..." Cotton didn't have to finish his sentence.

"It just can't end badly," Sam said. "It just can't. He's worked so hard."

"You know them bank folks. Whadda you think?"

"I think we've done the best we could. All we could."

"And if that ain't good enough?" Mamie asked.

Sam shook her head. She couldn't bear the thought that everything they had done would be for nothing. God, she wished the phone would ring and it would be over.

"Well." Cotton sighed and tossed down the last of his coffee. "Reckon I'll go see if Ryder needs help." And he left.

Mamie watched him go then turned to Sam. "I been keepin' an eye on you and Ryder the last coupla days. Somethin's different, and I ain't jest talkin' about you agreein' to work for him."

Sam knew Mamie liked her, but she also knew her loyalty was to Ryder. She shrugged, tried to keep her face expressionless. "I don't know what you mean—"

"I mean you got it worse that I thought. You've done fallen for him. Fallen hard. This ain't no casual thing, is it?"

"Why would you think that?"

"You're plumb crazy 'bout that man and don't deny it. For sure and for certain. I told you once before I could see it in your face. Reckon I jest didn't know how serious it was."

"It's not serious—"

"It is for you, and you're worried sick he don't feel the same way. Ain't that right?"

Sam sighed. She'd never been very good at lying. "You win. I am crazy about him, and I am worried sick."

"I don't think you got cause."

"Why? Did Ryder say something? Did he—"

"No, but I told you somethin' was different lately. Mostly Ryder. He's—" she paused a moment "—calmer. Like he's finally found the thing that makes him complete. I'd say he's in love with you."

"Oh, Mamie. Do you really think so?"

"I do. Might not have hit him yet, but it's creepin' up on him, for sure."

Sam sat down, folded her hands in her lap. "I love him so much, I ache every time I look at him. He's the first thing I think about when I open my eyes and the last thing I think about before I close them. He's my dream, Mamie. All these years, I've held on to the dream that someday I'd find a man I could give all my love to. Ryder's the one. I love him with all my heart."

"Yeah," Mamie sighed. "I remember that feelin'. It's heaven and hell sorta mixed up together."

Sam smiled. "Exactly."

"I figured that's why you decided to stay."

"Wild horses couldn't make me leave him now."

IN THE BARN, Ryder worked over a quarter horse as if he planned to enter him in a national competition. He concentrated all his thoughts and energy on the horse to keep from thinking about what was really on his mind. Fear. Cold, stark, unadulterated fear. The day was almost half over, and every minute was pure agony waiting for the phone call that would decide his life. Looking back, he was glad his better judgment had prevailed and he hadn't blurted out his feelings for Sam. But he'd wanted to. He'd wanted to shout them from the cupola atop the barn rather than merely offer her a job. It was a good thing he hadn't. With every passing second fear that the bank would reject him grew, gnawed at his insides like a ravenous beast. What if he'd told her he loved her, then the loan was rejected? Would she feel sorry for him? Stay on out of pity? He couldn't bear that. Despite the fact that he was positive she had feelings for him, no woman could be expected to accept a man without a future. Movies and novels might proclaim two people could live on love, but reality told a different story. If he lost the ranch he would have nothing to offer her. And he had too much pride to go to her empty-handed.

Cotton came into the barn. "You gonna brush that horse's hair off right down to the hide."

"Just keeping busy."

"Well, why don't you—"

They both glanced up when Sam rushed into the barn. "Phone call," she said, almost out of breath. "It's the bank. You want me to transfer it to the office?" She pointed to the office/tack room at the end of the line of stalls.

"Yeah. No, wait! I'll go with you." He dropped the currycomb, and all three raced for the house.

Mamie was pacing the kitchen floor when the others

came tearing into the house. "They're still holdin'," she told them.

Ryder hesitated, then went into his office.

Sam had to fight the urge to follow him. Part of her desperately wanted to be with him, while another part knew he should receive the news alone. Especially if... No! She wouldn't think like that. Stay positive, she told herself, and pray.

"He's been in there a damned long time," Cotton said after only ten minutes.

"That's a good sign, right?" Mamie fiddled with a corner of her apron, rolling and unrolling it.

"Absolutely," Sam said. "They're probably discussing payment terms, and—"

Ryder walked into the room and stopped just inside the door. He simply stood there for a moment without saying a word.

Sam held her breath.

"No dice," was all he said. Then he crossed the kitchen in three long strides, yanked open the door and walked out.

9

THE THREE PEOPLE who loved Ryder Wells the most stared after him in stunned silence.

"Oh, God," Sam finally whispered.

Cotton jerked his weathered hat from his head and flung it to the floor. "Well, if that ain't the damnedest, meanest, most ignorant thing I ever heard tell of. Don't those jackasses know a good deal when they hear one? Don't they know a good man when they see one? I've a good mind to go up there to Dallas and tell those blind sons a bitches 'zactly what I think of 'em. Never in all my born days—"

"Cotton." Mamie put her hand on his arm. "That's what we all wanna do, but it won't do no good. Those people are only interested in money. Don't make no never mind that they jest ruined a man's life."

"She's right," Sam said, tears sliding down her face. "Their only consideration is the bottom line—the impressive figure they can print in their annual report. It's nothing personal, just business. I guarantee you they won't give what they did today another thought, much less lose any sleep over it. The file will be tossed into a stack, an official letter written, and that's that."

"Well, it ain't right." Cotton sniffed and turned

away before swiping at his face with the sleeve of his shirt. "It just ain't right."

Sam stood up, but her legs were wobbly. "I need to go to him."

"Wait a while," Mamie suggested. "Let him wrestle with it till he gets a good grip on it before you talk to him. His pride won't let him talk now."

Sam sat down, partly because of what Mamie had said and partly because she didn't know what to say to Ryder at the moment. Everything that came to mind sounded either so trite it was stupid or so Pollyanna it was ridiculous. How could she ask him to cheer up when there was very little to be cheery about? She remembered how desolation and isolation felt all too well. She'd only been a child when her aunt had to leave her at the orphanage, old enough to remember and young enough to still be comforted by caring words and hugs. Ryder was no child. And while caring words and caresses might help, they were far from a cure. Money wasn't everything, but in this case it was the only thing that could help.

"Maybe he asked for too much." Cotton retrieved his hat but didn't put it on. "Maybe if he went back and talked to 'em, settled for less money, they'd be more likely to listen."

"We cut it as thin as we dared," Sam said. "The entire proposal was absolutely cut to the bone. I don't know how, or where, we could take out anything else."

"Well," Mamie said, "he's jest gonna haveta sell some of the land to keep the rest. I know that's the last thing he wanted. But he won't let us help, won't take on a partner. What else can he do?" She turned to Sam. "How much would he haveta sell to make it work?"

"Rough estimate? It depends on what the market will bear, but I'd say at least a hundred acres."

Cotton glanced up. "That's damn near a third of the ranch."

Mamie sighed, pulled out a chair from the kitchen table and sat down. "Thank the good Lord a body can't build on nothing less than two acres in Copper Canyon. Least that'll keep out them throw-'em-up-fast-and-cheap builders."

"The neighbors ain't gonna like it if he sells," Cotton announced.

"The neighbors ain't in this fix," Mamie snapped.

"What about the neighborin' town then? They're tryin' to change the law so they can sell to them cheap developers. Got somethin' attached to that bond election that comes up next month. And it'll probably pass. How long you think it's gonna be before greed spreads? Copper Canyon already fought the city council on that same thing twice, but if another town knuckles under—"

"Can't do nothing 'bout that, Cotton. You know it, I know it, and Ryder knows it." Mamie slapped a hand to her knee. "You jest gotta go to him and *make* him let us help, and that's all there is to it. Remind him if he goes, we go, so we got, uh, whaddayacallit?"

"A vested interest," Sam said.

"Yeah. We got a vested interest in this place. Lived here most of our lives and sure planned on dyin' here."

"He wouldn't take it before, won't take it now," Cotton said.

"Well, things is different now. He's desperate."

"It ain't enough," Cotton told his wife.

"I know that. Probably no more than forty or fifty thousand. We could sell them stock things we was hangin' on to for retirement. Maybe bring it up to a hundred thousand."

Sam had been noticeably quiet, and Mamie turned to her. "Whatcha think?"

"I'm thinking about something Cotton said. There is a possibility, a very small possibility, that the bank might reconsider if the size of the loan was reduced. The day Ryder went to the bank he told me their biggest concern was the amount of money he asked for."

"You think they'd do it?"

"They might if the reduction was significant."

"And our piddly little dollars ain't enough. That what you're thinkin'?" Mamie asked.

"Yes, but I think I know where we can get enough to make it work."

"Where?"

"Me."

The other two stared at her, dumbfounded. "You?" Mamie finally said.

"Yes. I've got some land—"

"Oh, hold on there, missy." Cotton waved a hand in dismissal. "You talkin' 'bout them five acres you got?"

"Yes."

"Forget it. No way Ryder is gonna stand still for you sellin' yore dream to help him keep his."

"But I don't have to sell. Not if the bank will take the land as collateral, and there's no reason they shouldn't. It's mine free and clear."

"It don't make no difference. He's a proud man. He won't take it."

"What are the two of you talkin' about?" Mamie demanded.

After Cotton explained, she shook her head. "Cotton's right. He won't take it."

"Well, now." Cotton scratched his head. "Maybe we can sorta go at this thing through the back door. If I can badger Ryder into acceptin' help from me and Mamie, then maybe I can say we got a lot more for the stock than we figured and—"

"No, Cotton. As much as I want Ryder to accept our help, I won't lie to him and I won't try to manipulate him. If he found out, he might not forgive any of us." She shook her head. "No. I won't do that to you or him. Besides, there's no way it would work without Ryder's knowledge."

Mamie reached across the table and patted her hand. "You love him that much."

Sam stood, looked at her. "More. I need to call the bank, then I need to find Ryder."

Then she set out to do whatever she could to help the man she loved.

ONE BOOTED FOOT resting on the bottom rail of the corral, one arm resting on the top rail, Ryder stared into space. It was over. All over. He knew that. Logically, he knew that. The phone call from the bank had confirmed it. But why wasn't his brain getting through to his heart? He didn't want to look at what he was about to lose, but he couldn't close his eyes for fear it would be gone when he opened them. He didn't want to think about his future, but he couldn't stop dismal thoughts from bombarding him like a kamikaze attack. His mind, heart, his whole being were split between desperately clutching at his dying dream and facing the reality that waited for him like a stalking animal. Emotions seethed and bubbled inside him like a volcano on the verge of eruption. And he feared an explosion was inevitable.

"Ryder?"

He almost jumped at the sound of Sam's voice. He'd been so preoccupied he hadn't heard her walk up. Part of him resented her being there. Another part thanked heaven she was. Hurt, confused and desperate, he wanted to hold her to him and push her away at the same time. He felt like a man trying to walk over tissue paper stretched across the Grand Canyon.

"I'm not even going to ask if you're all right. You aren't."

"I will be." But he wasn't so sure. At the moment he was only sure that he'd given everything he had and it hadn't been enough. He had the uneasy feeling that his father, grandfather, all the Wellses from past generations, were looking down at him and hanging their heads in shame.

The desolation in his voice almost broke her heart. She knew what she had to say, to offer, wasn't going to be easy for him to accept, but she had to make him understand that he wasn't alone, that the situation wasn't hopeless.

"I know how much this place means to you. Believe it or not, it's come to mean a lot to me in the short time since I arrived. I've been happier and felt more secure here than any place I've ever known. You've let me be a part of your dream, and I'm grateful. That's why I've done something to help you keep it."

"Sam—"

"This may not be the way you wanted, but it is a way for you to have what you want, so just hear me out."

She didn't want to come right out and say, "I fixed it," and she didn't want it to look like charity. Sam took a deep breath and proceeded carefully into the explanation she hoped he would understand and accept. "After you left I called the bank. I told the loan officer I was your office manager and asked if they would reconsider the loan if we either reduced the amount or found sufficient collateral to offset a big portion of the money. They agreed to look at a revised proposal under those conditions."

"I'm not following. How can I reduce the amount, Sam? You know yourself how close we figured everything. And as far as collateral goes, what collateral? Short of selling off a huge chunk of the land I'm trying to save, they've got everything of value I own. There *is* no collateral."

"Cotton and Mamie want to make you a loan that will help reduce it. And—" she rushed on when he started to speak "—they won't take no for an answer. Both of them want to live out the rest of their lives here and consider it just plain good sense. They're going to badger you until you accept, so you might as well give in gracefully."

"That's generous, but it still doesn't—"

"As for the collateral, I know someone with five acres of prime property near McKinney, free and clear. And willing to invest—"

"No!"

"But, Ryder, there're no strings attached, I promise. The last appraisal put the value close to four hundred thousand, but the loan officer told me it might be worth more. He said in the last four months property values in that area have skyrocketed, and he wouldn't be surprised if the land was worth closer to a half a million dollars. Between Mamie and Cotton's money and using the deed for collateral—"

"I can't believe you." He'd been listening to her but still couldn't believe his ears. The only thing he knew for certain was that she'd done what he couldn't. He should have been thrilled, overjoyed, over the moon with relief and happiness. But he wasn't. It didn't make any sense, but suddenly the volcano erupted, triggering the waiting explosion. There had been no hope, then she came along and gave him hope. Then hope was snatched away, and now here she was again, waving faith and second chances under his nose like a seductive perfume. She had rescued him, bailed him out, by doing exactly what he didn't want. And she'd put him between a rock and a hard place. If he didn't accept, he would lose everything. If he did, he might lose control of the ranch, his life.

"I called the bank—"

"And took it upon yourself to negotiate another deal." The words were out before he could stop them, then discovered he didn't want to. All the anger, frustration and wounded pride boiled up inside him and spilled out.

"I—I only wanted—"

"Just what exactly is it you want?"

Stunned at his attitude, it took her a second to realize he must be in the throes of some sort of emotional whiplash. With all the stress of the last few months, worrying over bankruptcy, who could blame him for popping his cork a little? "To help," she said, keeping her voice as calm as possible.

"I told you I didn't want a partner, and what did you do? You stepped in without even asking me."

"I was afraid you'd say no." Out of love and her eagerness to help him, she'd made a grave error in judgment. How could she have lost sight of the fact that trust was so important?

"Damn straight. But you ignored that and just went right on, didn't you?"

"Yes, but—"

"But what I want doesn't count?"

"Of course, it counts."

"Then why, Sam? Why would you do such a thing?"

"I'm sorry. I should have talked to you first. But I believe in you and I want you to have your dream so much that I—I acted without thinking."

"Don't you see? If I have to share it with someone else, it isn't mine. And what if I fail—"

"You won't. I know you won't."

"How do you know?"

"Because I love you." She hadn't intended to blurt it out that way, but it was the truth, and the reason she'd done what she had. "I love you. As crazy as it sounds, I think I've loved you almost from the first. And because I love you I understand that you feel you've got to prove to your father *and* your brother that you're as good as they were. You've got to do it all by yourself or it's just not any good."

Her words held up a mirror to his pride, and he didn't like the image reflected back at him. It was almost as if she'd had a glimpse into his soul and seen his hidden torment. He felt raw, exposed, and he hated it. So he lashed out.

"You expect me to believe you did all this out of love?"

"It's true."

"I wonder, is it love or a way to buy yourself a family, a home? Is that it, Sam? Is that your cut for finding me a partner I don't want?"

Sam reeled as if she'd been struck. He might as well have struck her. A blow couldn't have inflicted any more pain than his words had.

"I did it because I love you. And I thought, hoped, that maybe, possibly, you could love me back."

Her words echoed his own thoughts so much that he winced. It was too good to be true. Too convenient. He couldn't trust it.

"I didn't know I was such a threat to your precious

ego and pride," she said, shaking her head in frustration.

"You talk about ego and pride. You just took it upon yourself—"

"Don't you get it? I'm not interested in taking. I want to give. That's what love is about, isn't it? And you're right. I do want a home, a family and as much happiness as I can cram into one lifetime. I thought I'd found it through sheer, dumb luck, but obviously, I was wrong. I should have remembered that you'd go down in flames before you took on a partner." Tears flowed unchecked down her cheeks. "It's not that you don't want to accept help. You can't. Well, you don't have to worry, Ryder. I'll make sure the investor has no claim over your precious ranch and signs whatever piece of paper your lawyers create saying so. All I care about now is that Cotton and Mamie are okay. See, when I make a deal, I stick to it." With that she turned and walked away.

Ryder watched her cross the lawn to the house and go inside. He felt as if his heart had just been ripped from his chest. An hour ago he'd thought he wanted to spend the rest of his life with Sam, and now... He looked around at his home, his land and felt physically sick. His whole life had gone horribly wrong in a matter of minutes, and she was at the heart of it. How could she have gone over his head, so to speak, when she knew how he felt about anyone trying to take control of his business? How could she do that, then say she did it for love? That wasn't love, that was—

He heard the kitchen door slam, looked up and saw

Sam walk out, heading toward the back of the barn where her car and his truck were parked. She was leaving. And he was torn between wanting to turn away and wanting to run after her. Instead, he walked to the house. Cotton and Mamie were in the kitchen together.

"She's done left," Cotton said.

"I saw her."

"Did you see she was cryin'?"

Ryder knew he'd been cruel, and part of him wanted to take it back, but it was too late. He felt betrayed, disillusioned in a way that had little to do with losing the ranch and everything to do with losing what he thought he'd found in Sam.

"Said she'd send for whatever was left here," Cotton told him.

"Fine. I'm going to my office."

"Not so damned fast," Mamie said when he turned to leave. "I wanna know what you said to her."

"She didn't tell you?"

"Hell no, she was cryin' too hard to get out a word. Which don't make any sense 'cause when she went to find you she was happy as a lark."

"Did she tell you she dug up some rich investor? The very thing she knew I didn't want. The jerk probably hopes I'll fail so he'll have a tax write-off. And for all I know she's been working toward this since the day she got here."

"And I suppose you told her that?"

"Words to that effect," Ryder huffed.

"Did you think to ask who this investor was?"

"Doesn't matter."

Mamie looked at Cotton. "Guess we didn't pray hard enough." Then she looked at Ryder. "Sounds to me like you been shootin' off your mouth and cuttin' your own throat in the process."

"Now hold on. I don't think—"

"At least we agree on somethin'. You ain't thinkin', period."

"Mamie, I know you like Sam, but she didn't belong here."

"Oh, she didn't, did she?"

"You don't understand. We made a stupid deal, and—"

"The only deal I see is that you got the appraisal gone, and she got a job tryin' to save your butt. You got the best damned thing to ever come down the pike, and she got dumped. Some deal, all right."

"She'll find something else for herself. She's good at it."

"Like findin' you someone to put money into your ranch? Like maybe givin' up her own dream to do it?"

"What are you talkin' about?"

"You tell 'im," she said to Cotton. "I don't like talkin' to a jackass."

"Sam owns that land, Ryder. She's the investor. Paid off them five acres all by herself. Told me it was the only place she'd ever felt like she belonged till she came here. I reckon that woman jest plain loves you to distraction."

Mamie walked to Ryder, put her hands on her hips and narrowed her gaze directly at him. "What size boots you wearin' these days?"

"Elevens, why?"

"Smile."

Still stunned at Cotton's words, he tried but only ended up with his mouth gaping open. Mamie turned her head one way then the other looking at his mouth. "Yep. I'd say they're a perfect fit." And she walked out of the kitchen.

A few seconds later, Cotton followed her, shaking his head as he went.

Ryder stood there, alone, knowing his life was in a shambles and it was by his own hand. For a grown man, he'd acted like the biggest idiot in six counties. And an ungrateful idiot, to boot. As he had for most of the bad moments in his life, he'd covered his fear and pain with anger. It was an old and costly behavior pattern. This time it had probably cost him Sam.

Ryder called himself several kinds of fool, plus some other names unsuitable for decent company. Not that he could put himself in the decent category with any assurance. The truth, when he finally faced it, was that he'd been so busy feeling sorry for himself, being angry at himself, he'd taken it out on the first person to cross his path. A person who didn't deserve it. Thinking back to the awful, hurtful things he'd said made him feel sick at his stomach. How could he have been so cruel?

Maybe because she'd been right. So dead-on right.

But that didn't give him the right to dump on her the way he had, he thought as he headed toward his truck. He had allowed the weight of four generations, and the warped idea that he had to be the son his father lost, to make him blind to his own strength and creativity. He had struggled for years to make something work that wasn't in his true heart. He loved the land as much as his father and brother had, but not the same way. Like his father and grandfather before him, Cliff had been born with the heart of a rancher. Ryder hadn't. His entire life had been the story of a square peg trying to fit into a round hole, and after Cliff died, he'd tried even harder. But it hadn't worked. Then he'd gone away thinking that was the solution, and it might have been if his dad hadn't died and handed over the legacy of Copper Canyon. Back to the round hole. Back to working to round off the corners of himself in order to fit. He'd had to do it, and do it alone.

Sam had seen through him like wet tissue paper. And for one ugly moment, he'd resented her insight to the point of blaming her. God, what a fool he was. What a blind, hardheaded, self-centered fool.

He only hoped it hadn't cost him the woman he loved. He knew what he had to do to try to make things right between him and Sam. Beg. For forgiveness. For a second chance. And keep on begging if he had to. For as long as it took.

SAM HADN'T BEEN headed in any particular direction when she walked out of the house. She just wanted a moment alone. When she ended up standing in front of her car, she was surprised. Had she subconsciously thought about leaving? A momentary urge to get away from the pain was understandable. It wouldn't work, of course, and she had no intention of walking away. The old Sam, the woman she'd been before coming to Copper Canyon, might have walked away from the pain of loving Ryder. But she wasn't that woman anymore. In truth, she never had been, not deep down where it counted. Besides, no matter where she went she couldn't stop loving him. It was pointless to try.

And deep in her heart she knew she didn't even want to try. She couldn't, wouldn't, give up on their love.

Her whole life had changed the day she made her deal with Ryder, and so had his, whether he wanted to admit it or not. She knew his words were born out of pain and a desperate need to be what was expected of him. God knew she'd struggled under the same burden for years. But sooner or later the burden became so heavy you either threw it off or buckled under the weight. And it would take a lot more than defensive words to make her buckle.

She was going to fight for what she wanted. And she was going to make Ryder fight, whether he wanted to or not. He had no right to give up on them. No matter what it took, she would make him see that what they had was too precious, too real, to lose. She turned to go to the house and ran smack dab into Ryder.

"Sam! I thought you'd gone."

"Not until I tell you what's on my mind. Now you listen to me, Ryder Wells. I'm not going to let you get away with this. It's too important, and I intend to say what I should have said to you hours ago."

"Go ahead. I was too blind to realize how much I loved you until it was too late. I deserve everything you can throw at me, plus some."

"You've got some nerve giving— What?"

"What?"

"What did you just say?"

"That I deserve—"

"No, before."

"You probably don't want to hear it. You probably wanna bash my head in for the way—"

"Did you say you loved me?"

"I wouldn't blame you if you threw it—"

"Ryder."

"—right back in my face—'

"Ryder!"

"What?"

"Say it." She held her breath, her heart beating fast as a drumroll.

"I love you, Sam. More than I ever thought possible. So much it scares me."

She sighed, relief and joy flowing through her like warm brandy. It was all right to be scared. They had that in common. "Why? I ask only because I'm scared, too."

"You are?"

She smiled. "It was okay to want you, but I was afraid to love you. Afraid to love. The smartest thing I ever did was make a deal with you."

He grinned, hope inching into his heart. "Told you it was gutsy."

"So, why are you scared?"

"Because you saw right through me. You knew I'd worked myself crazy because of my father and brother. And hearing you say it made me face the fact that everything—business falling off, getting behind on the loan payments—was because I've always blamed myself for not being like them. For not being them. Somehow I felt I had failed four generations. Then you came along with the most obvious solution, and I failed again. You're right. I've got some nerve giving you grief when I couldn't take it myself."

"You didn't let me finish."

"Are you finished, Sam? Are we finished?"

"I started to say that you had some nerve giving up.

On the ranch. On the possibility of us. I know you've had good reasons not to trust any woman, especially as a partner, but I'm not part of your past. I want to be part of your future. And you can't get rid of me so easy."

"I can't? I mean, I don't want to," he said, a little dazed but filled with shining hope.

She wrapped her arms around his neck. "In fact, I'm not moving an inch until I've convinced you of how much I love you."

He pulled her into a fierce embrace. "You don't have to convince me, and I'll never let you leave. I need you, Sam, and I love you so much. Can you forgive me?"

She took his face in her hands. "I already have."

"There's one more thing?"

"Anything."

"I'm looking for a partner. Someone looking to invest in a start-up stunt school and a hardheaded cowboy. Know anyone who might be interested in a lifetime commitment?"

"I think I can put you in touch with the perfect person...for just the right deal," she murmured, touching her lips to his.

10

"YOU'RE GONNA strain your eyes lookin' at that screen for hours on end." Hands on hips, Mamie shook her head. "Sides, it's nearly dark. Can't you pull yourself away from them numbers long enough to eat?"

"I just want to be sure I haven't made any mistakes, transposed any numbers. This report to the bank is too important." Sam stretched, pushed her chair away from the computer and rubbed her eyes. "But I am hungry. What have you got?"

"Chicken 'n' dumplin's," Mamie announced, then turned and headed for the kitchen.

Sam groaned. "I'm gaining weight faster than a prize pig."

"You could use it," Mamie called from the hall.

It had been a solid year of watching every expenditure down to the penny, and a lot of fattening food, Sam thought, gazing at the numbers on the screen. But it had been worth it. They were breaking even and just around the corner from a profit.

With the deed for the McKinney property, they had managed to secure the reorganizational loan and within sixty days had signed up their first five students. They were up to twenty-three, with plans in motion to expand the curriculum plus add a three-week limited session for amateurs, designed to be a sort of summer camp for stunt wannabes. They were still a long way from the milk-and-honey point, but they were getting there. Sam smiled, touched the simple gold band Ryder had slipped onto her finger the day they married. That, too, was a solid year ago.

"Partners," she whispered, so proud of everything they had accomplished. Then she rested her hand on her still relatively flat stomach. And everything they were going to accomplish.

"Sam?" Ryder called from the kitchen.

"Coming." She stood up, stretched again and went to join her family, and was greeted the instant she stepped into the kitchen.

"Surprise!"

Ryder, Cotton and Mamie stood around the table, which was set with the good china. Four wineglasses were already filled and waiting, along with a cake that had one huge lighted candle stuck in the middle.

"What's all this?" she asked as Ryder slipped an arm around her waist and kissed her.

"Celebration, sugar."

Ryder led Sam to the table, handed everyone a glass, then lifted his. "To hard work and a great family. The Copper Canyon Stunt School couldn't exist or grow without them." Then he turned to Sam. "And to my wife. The best business manager and deal maker on the planet."

"Hey," Sam said after taking a sip from her glass, "this isn't wine. It's cranberry juice. What gives?"

Ryder took the glass from her. "Pregnant women

aren't supposed to consume alcohol," he said, waiting for her reaction.

Her eyes widened. "How did you know?"

"Well, I've become much more aware since you came into my life. I'm not the same bullheaded cowboy you—"

"The doctor's office called," Cotton interrupted, grinning. "You forgot your stash of them prenuptial vitamins."

"Prenatal," Mamie corrected.

Sam barely heard her. She was too busy gazing into the eyes of the man she loved, the father of her baby. "Surprised?"

"Floored." His grin was as wide as Cotton's. "It's...wonderful. You're wonderful." He kissed her gently, softly, but as usual the kiss deepened. "I love you so much, Sam. I can't imagine what my life would be without you, and now to have a son—"

"It might be a girl."

"Okay by me." Ryder pulled Sam into his arms. "I'm crazy about the idea of a little girl, especially if she grows up to be like her mother."

Mamie nudged Cotton, signaling it was time to exit for a while, and they quietly slipped out the back door.

Sam looked into her husband's eyes, her heart so full of love and happiness it felt too small to contain it. "Who would have thought all of this could come from a simple deal?"

"I don't know about simple, but it was the best— No, *you're* the best deal I ever made," he said, and sealed it with a kiss.

HARLEQUIN®

Temptation.

It's hot...and it's out of control!

This spring, the forecast is hot and steamy!
Don't miss these bold, provocative, ultra-sexy books!

PRIVATE INVESTIGATIONS by Tori Carrington
April 2002
Secretary-turned-P.I. Ripley Logan never thought her first job
would have her running for her life—or crawling into
a stranger's bed....

ONE HOT NUMBER by Sandy Steen
May 2002
Accountant Samantha Collins may be good with numbers, but
she needs some work with men...until she meets sexy but
broke rancher Ryder Wells. Then she decides to make him a
deal—her brains for his bed. Sam's getting the better of the
deal, but hey, who's counting?

WHAT'S YOUR PLEASURE? by Julie Elizabeth Leto
June 2002
Mystery writer Devon Michaels is in a bind. Her publisher has
promised her a lucrative contract, *if* she makes the jump to
erotic thrillers. The problem: Devon can't write a love scene to
save her life. Luckily for her, Detective Jake Tanner is an
expert at "hands-on" training....

Don't miss this thrilling threesome!

HARLEQUIN®
Makes any time special ®

Visit us at www.eHarlequin.com

HTH

HARLEQUIN®
Temptation.

Look for bed, breakfast and more...!

COOPER'S CORNER

Some of your favorite Temptation authors are checking in early at Cooper's Corner Bed and Breakfast

In May 2002:

#877 *The Baby and the Bachelor*
Kristine Rolofson

In June 2002:

#881 *Double Exposure*
Vicki Lewis Thompson

In July 2002:

#885 *For the Love of Nick*
Jill Shalvis

In August 2002 things heat up even more at Cooper's Corner. There's a whole year of intrigue and excitement to come—twelve fabulous books bound to capture your heart and mind!

Join all your favorite Harlequin authors in Cooper's Corner!

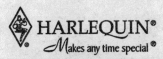

HARLEQUIN®
Makes any time special®

Visit us at www.eHarlequin.com

HTCC

Pure page-turning passionate pleasure is here with this provocative collection!

Bedazzled

by *New York Times* bestselling author

JAYNE ANN KRENTZ

And bestselling Harlequin®
Temptation authors

VICKI LEWIS THOMPSON

RITA CLAY ESTRADA

Three sensual authors bring you the captivating *Montclair Emeralds* trilogy in a special anthology brimming with romance, passion and mystery! At the heart of each of these provocative stories is a priceless piece of jewelry that becomes a talisman for true love for each couple.

Coming in June 2002.

HARLEQUIN®
Makes any time special®

Visit us at www.eHarlequin.com

PHB

eHARLEQUIN.com

| community | membership |
| buy books | authors | online reads | magazine | learn to write |

magazine

♥—————————————————— **quizzes**

Is he the one? What kind of lover are you? Visit the **Quizzes** area to find out!

♥—————————————— **recipes for romance**

Get scrumptious meal ideas with our **Recipes for Romance**.

♥—————————————— **romantic movies**

Peek at the **Romantic Movies** area to find Top 10 Flicks about First Love, ten Supersexy Movies, and more.

♥———————————————— **royal romance**

Get the latest scoop on your favorite royals in **Royal Romance**.

♥——————————————————— **games**

Check out the **Games** pages to find a ton of interactive romantic fun!

♥——————————————— **romantic travel**

In need of a romantic rendezvous? Visit the **Romantic Travel** section for articles and guides.

♥———————————————— **lovescopes**

Are you two compatible? Click your way to the **Lovescopes** area to find out now!

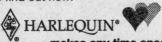

HARLEQUIN®

makes any time special—online...

Visit us online at
www.eHarlequin.com

HINTMAG

Back by popular request...
those amazing Buckhorn Brothers!

*Once
and Again*

Containing two full-length novels by
the Queen of Sizzle,

USA Today bestselling author

LORI
FOSTER

They're all gorgeous, all sexy and all single...at least for now!
This special volume brings you the sassy and seductive
stories of Sawyer and Morgan Buckhorn—offering you
hours of *hot, hot* reading!

Available in June 2002 wherever books are sold.

And in September 2002 look for FOREVER AND ALWAYS,
containing the stories of Gabe and Jordan Buckhorn!

HARLEQUIN®
Makes any time special ®

Visit us at www.eHarlequin.com

PHLF-1R

HARLEQUIN®

Temptation

THE WRONG BED

What happens when a girl finds herself in the
wrong bed...with the *right* guy?

Find out in:

#866 NAUGHTY BY NATURE by Jule McBride
February 2002

#870 SOMETHING WILD by Toni Blake
March 2002

#874 CARRIED AWAY by Donna Kauffman
April 2002

#878 HER PERFECT STRANGER by Jill Shalvis
May 2002

#882 BARELY MISTAKEN by Jennifer LaBrecque
June 2002

#886 TWO TO TANGLE by Leslie Kelly
July 2002

Midnight mix-ups have never been so much fun!

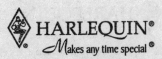

HARLEQUIN®
Makes any time special ®

Visit us at www.eHarlequin.com

HTNBN2